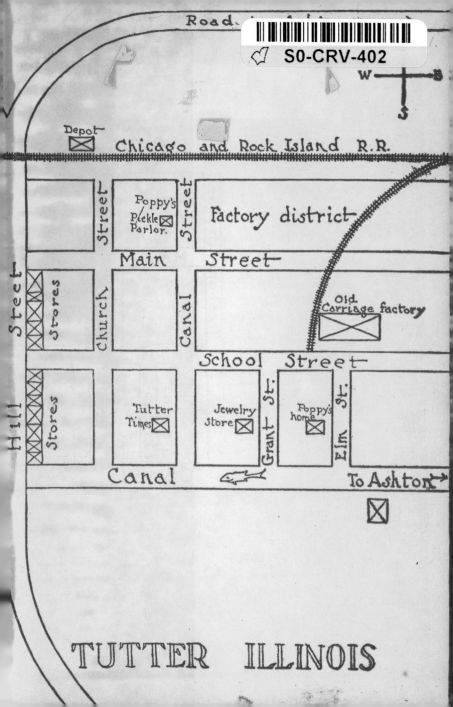

JERRY TODD,
PIRATE

BOY, YOU SHOULD HAVE HEARD OUR PEACHY WAR WHOOPS.

Jerry Todd Pirate.   *Frontispiece (Page 25)*

JERRY TODD, PIRATE

BY

LEO EDWARDS

AUTHOR OF

THE JERRY TODD BOOKS

THE POPPY OTT BOOKS

GROSSET & DUNLAP

PUBLISHERS   : :   NEW YORK

It is to the particular Boy Scout in our own family, and to his doughty scouting pals, the Boy Scouts of Cambridge, Wisconsin, fine, trusty fellows all of them, and good men in the making, that this skylarking tale of outdoor life, with its swashbuckling piratical atmosphere, is affectionately dedicated.

GREETINGS, FELLOW GOLDFISH MEMBERS!

So far Jerry Todd has accommodatingly written the prefaces of these books, of which this particular volume is the eighth in order of publication, the preceding volumes having the titles:

JERRY TODD AND THE WHISPERING MUMMY
JERRY TODD AND THE ROSE-COLORED CAT
JERRY TODD AND THE OAK ISLAND TREASURE
JERRY TODD AND THE WALTZING HEN
JERRY TODD AND THE TALKING FROG
JERRY TODD AND THE PURRING EGG
JERRY TODD IN THE WHISPERING CAVE

But our skylarking young "pirate" is going to be relieved here of a job that he never particularly liked. I am going to write this preface myself. Not that I hope to improve on our fluent young scribe's style. As a matter of fact, I like his breezy, happy-go-lucky "lingo" immensely. And I dare say you do, too.

But I have something special to say, as the author of the Jerry Todd and Poppy Ott books, about our new "Freckled Goldfish" lodge. Is that name familiar to you? It is to a great many boys. For our membership is growing rapidly. Here in Cambridge where I live the postmaster frequently says to me: "Mr. Edwards, you get a *lot* of letters." And I think my face shines like a big red prune (if there is such a thing) when I tell him, with pride, that the big bulk of these letters are from the young readers of my books.

Boys living near here, who read the manuscript of "Poppy Ott and the Freckled Goldfish" before that book was published, asked me eagerly if I cared if they got up a real secret lodge, like Poppy's, as featured in the book's seventh chapter.

That gave me an idea. Why not go my enthusiastic young friends one better, I thought, and get up a widely extended secret "fun" lodge, open to all Jerry Todd and Poppy Ott fans everywhere?

So we started the lodge, telling boys about it in the preface of the "Freckled Goldfish" book. And the response was wonderful. I never realized before how many thousands of loyal pals Jerry and Poppy had. The letters simply poured in. Letters from big boys, small boys, freckled boys, good-looking boys, pug-

nosed boys, skinny boys, fat boys, sawed-offs
and bean-poles. Girls even wrote. Not bean-
poles, of course, for we never would call any
little girl a bean-pole. But the girls wrote, just
the same. Which, of course, was all right.

These letters principally were applications
for life membership in our new lodge. Yet I
received many special letters. And how much I
enjoyed these—all of the letters, in fact—you
can't imagine. Maybe some of you boys think
an author, even though he specializes in boys'
books, doesn't care to read letters from scattered boys whose only claim on his friendship
is their interest in his stories. To cite my own
case, you may think that book writing with
me is just a business. In other words, having done the ''job,'' as you might say, I would
prefer not to be bothered by boys.

As a matter of fact, there is nothing in this
world, including wealth, swell automobiles,
gingersnaps and everything else, that I prize
as highly as the friendship and companionship
of boys. I read every letter that I receive.
And every letter is answered. Of course, I
don't write personal letters to all of the boys
joining our lodge. We have a special printed
letter for that. But when a boy asks me a
question, that question is answered, with a pen,

on the margin of the printed letter. And in some cases I write separate personal letters. I don't *dictate* these letters: I pound them out with my own "mitts." I mention this, for I want you to realize fully how much I value the friendship that your bully good letters have made possible.

In writing to me you need never worry about your commas and periods. Just forget that I am an "author." I really don't know half as much as some boys think I do. If you want to spell "cat" with a capital "K," that's all right with me. The main point is that you thought enough of my books to want to write and tell me about it. Therefore every word that you write is appreciated for the fine friendly thought behind it. Through fooling around with boys, and writing books for boys, I think I have come to understand boys quite well. I never tire of them. In fact, I go out of my way every day to be with them. Their fun is my fun. I haven't a single interest in which boys are left out. The more I see of them the better I like them, and the deeper I realize how fortunate I am in having their complete confidence.

Many boys generously send me snapshots of themselves, for which I am grateful. I'm told

things—close to the writer's heart—in strict
confidence. One boy aspires to be a writer—
and will I please tell him how I got started.
Another boy (who probably likes pie!) wants
to be a baker. I get letters from hospitals,
written by boys who cannot walk. These letters touch my heart. For I would wish that
the lives of all boys could be constantly filled
with sunshine and laughter. So I am always
grateful that my stories of fun and mystery are
bringing some small joy into the lives of these
shut-ins, who never will be able to swim, to
wade in mud puddles or play the rollicking
games so dear to boys and so necessary in their
development.

And having thus extensively expressed my
earnest appreciation, I'd like to leave the
thought with you, in case you are *not* a member
of "The Secret and Mysterious Order of the
Freckled Goldfish," that we're eagerly waiting
for you to join. The whole purpose of the
"lodge" is to provide added fun for boys. So
every Jerry Todd and Poppy Ott fan ought to
join. If you are too busy to write, ask Mother
or Dad to write for you. Or maybe Mother
will write and surprise you with your membership card. We have a big registration book
here, in which are recorded the names and ad-

dresses of all members. I think you will be proud to have your name in this book.

Then, too, as I have mentioned, each new member receives a unique numbered membership card, designed by Bert Salg, the popular illustrator of these books. Containing a comical picture of Poppy's "Freckled Goldfish," together with our secret rules, each card also bears my own personal autograph, if that is of any importance to you.

Any boy anywhere, of any age, size or color, who has a friendly feeling toward Jerry and Poppy, is welcome to join. It will cost you two two-cent United States postage stamps—four cents in all. One red stamp will pay the postage on your membership card; and the other stamp will partly cover the cost of the envelope and the illustrated card.

In applying for membership please observe these simple rules:

(1) Print or write your name plainly.
(2) Supply your complete address.
(3) Give your age.
(4) Enclose two two-cent United States postage stamps—or four one-cent stamps.
(5) Address your letter to,

Leo Edwards,
Cambridge, Wisconsin.

And bear in mind, too, that I'm always mighty glad to have my young readers drop in on me at Hi-Lee Cottage, our summer home at Lake Ripley, just out of Cambridge. Boys never lack a welcome here, as many hundreds of boys already know. There's no formality. We prefer to be plainly friendly instead.

THE AUTHOR

CONTENTS

JERRY TODD, PIRATE

CHAPTER I

MRS. CASSIDY'S SPOOKY STORY

Now that we had an island of our own, just like Robinson Crusoe, the proper thing for us to do, Scoop Ellery said in good leadership, was to stock it up with animals.

So at his directions we started out with marbles and other truck to see what we could find. The first day, working in pairs, Scoop and I on the north side of town, as it is divided by the Tutter canal, and Peg Shaw and Red Meyers, our chums, on the south side, we traded for seven dogs, thirteen cats, three guinea pigs, three tame rabbits, a pair of white mice, a sick hen and a three-legged squirrel.

We were particularly pleased over the cats. And our big hope was that each one of them would get busy, in its new home, and raise a hundred kittens.

Later on, as the kittens and grand-kittens and great-grand-kittens grew up and got married, we could go into the fur business, killing off ten or twenty thousand full-grown cats a

1

season, which, at fifty cents a pelt, say, would give us a very nice income. And we could sell rabbit skins, too—probably a thousand or more each year. We sure were the lucky little things, all right.

No wonder the Stricker gang looked at us kind of envious-like. For they had heard about our island, and how we were going to live in a cave like Robinson Crusoe, with goat skins for pants—only we probably would have to make our pants out of cat skins. But that was all right. Cat skins ought to make swell pants. In the winter we could wear the fur on the inside, if it didn't tickle, and in hot weather, like it was now, we could turn our pants inside out. Or, for that matter, having the lonely canal island all to ourselves, we could go without pants.

Mrs. Ellery didn't like it very well when she came home from a card party and found her basement full of strange cats and dogs. So, secretly throwing out the marmalade that one of the cats had stepped in, we moved all of our animals into Red's big barn, kind of keeping the cats and dogs separated. They'd be nice to each other when they got acquainted, just like Robinson Crusoe's cats and dogs. But just now their main ambition seemed to be to want to chew each other up.

The next morning, after burying the hen under a gooseberry bush, the poor thing having passed away during the night, we started out again, Red having the good fortune just before noon to fall in with a gypsy who sold him a gray horse, with a tail and everything, for only five dollars, which, as you probably will agree with me, was a big bargain.

Of course, old Chris wasn't the best-looking horse in the world. We couldn't expect that . . . not for five dollars. But he was a nice horse, just the same. His feet were big, Red said, passing along the gypsy's story to us, because he had the dropsy. Poor thing! Our hearts were touched by the beseeching look in his meek eyes. He seemed to realize how shabby he looked, with his big hairy feet, scraggly gray mane and caved-in back. And he was afraid, I guess, in his timid way, that we wouldn't love him. But, to that point, we would have loved him no matter how he looked, for the one thing we needed, above all else, was a horse.

Having picked up an old surrey on another trade, it was our plan to use this in hauling our truck to Oak Island, there being a reason, as I'll explain later on, why we preferred to go by road. So, when dinner was over we got our stuff together, putting the cats in a big crate, which was tied on behind. The mice didn't take up much room. Nor the guinea pigs. I forgot where we put the rabbits. But everything was taken care of. Then, with the dogs tied behind, each to a separate rope, and the canopy top loaded down with pillows and bedding, we started out, Red and Peg in the front seat, with Mr. Meyers' tool chest between them, and Scoop and I in the back seat, one holding the boiled ham that our folks had generously contributed, and the other the bag of tinware. Of course, as soon as we got settled on our island we'd make some nice clay dishes, like Robinson Crusoe's, but we had to have something to start with.

As could be expected, Bid Stricker and his gang made fun of us. Jealous over our good fortune they called our nice horse an old crowbait, asking us jeering-like, as they followed us to the edge of town, why we didn't go into the laundry business, using the horse's ribs for a washboard.

And not satisfied with insulting us they started pegging stuff at us. We piled out then. And when we came back, after chasing them home, we found Christopher Columbus, which was the horse's full name, sound asleep in Mrs. Dexter's big pansy bed.

Mrs. Dexter is the wealthy widow who buys

old dishes. That's her hobby. Raised in Tutter, she spent her married life in Chicago, where her husband, a barber in the Board of Trade district, made a big fortune by quizzing his customers for market tips. When she came back to Tutter to live, following her husband's death, the Stitch and Chatter Club, of which Mother is a member, got up a swell reception. But to the disappointment of the stitchers and chatterers who had expected the wealthy widow to be the final word in style, Mrs. Dexter, though appreciative, made it plain to her neighbors that she wasn't interested in society. Her big interest, she explained, was in antiques, particularly old dishes.

You probably wouldn't believe me if I were to tell you how many thousands of dollars she has spent on old dishes, gathered from all over the world. She goes to Europe every year. And her combined pottery and china collection, I've been told, is one of the finest in the country. But she never uses these dishes. She keeps them in locked cabinets. And what good they are to her I can't see. But if she wants to spend her money that way, rich as she is, I suppose it's nobody's business but her own.

Mother still laughs about the party. For Mrs. Dexter's parent, an old Irish lady who earlier lived in Tutter, came into the room, where the ladies were playing bridge, wearing her wig hind-side-foremost. Of course, everybody present knew that old Mrs. Cassidy had completely lost her hair from putting something on it in the dark that wasn't hair tonic, but, even so, the stylish Tutter ladies, who were trying to show off and act the way they had expected the wealthy city woman to act, felt that it would be terribly embarrassing to the guest of honor to see her talkative mother with the tail end of her wig hanging down in front. And to make matters worse, to the view of some, the old lady told how glad she was to get back to the country where she could raise a pig. Home didn't seem the same, she said, recalling the early days of her married life, without a pig. Pressed into a card game, she lost her temper and kicked the table over. Then, getting up a sweat, she yanked the wig off altogether, hanging it on a doorknob. According to Mother's report, the Tutter women, for the most part, were shocked speechless. But Mrs. Dexter just laughed, realizing, I guess, that she and her mother were rich enough to do as they pleased without fear of the neighbors' talk.

Some people, when they get a little money, think it's smart to put on airs. But not Mrs. Dexter. She even does her own housework. Outside of this silly notion of hers of collecting old dishes, I think she's all right. Certainly, I'd rather go to her house, where a fellow is sure of getting something good to eat, than to some of the other swell places that I know of, where the only thing you get is a cold reminder to clean your feet at the door. This "style" stuff that so many of the women talk about makes me sick. Why, I know one kid in Tutter whose mother makes him wear a white shirt and a necktie every day in the week. It's *stylish*, she says. Just think of that! And I absolutely know that the poor kid never went barefooted in his life.

Well, being friends of Mrs. Dexter's, we felt pretty badly about her wrecked pansy bed. And much as we loved Christopher Columbus we gave him a good talking to. It was all right for him to take a nap, we said, but he should know better than to squat in a nice pansy bed. I'm sure he understood what we were saying to him. For his eyes got sadder than ever. So, for fear that he might start crying, and thus make himself sick, we quit scolding him.

Having volunteered to get a strap to repair our broken harness, I ran around to the back door, where I found Mrs. Dexter opening a box that had just been delivered to her by the express company. And what do you suppose was in the box. Another dish!

"Oh! . . ." cried the collector, sort of hugging the tacky-looking dish to her heart. "Isn't it a *darling?* I saw it in a private collection the last time I was in Boston. And I was *so* afraid that some one else might get it ahead of me. . . . Mother dear," she then called into the kitchen, where the elder was at work, "are any of the fried cakes ready? Jerry's here."

Fried cakes! Boy, if there's anything I love it's fried cakes . . . especially the kind that Mrs. Cassidy makes.

Seated in the cozy kitchen, with six fried cakes in my lap, on a plate, I told Mrs. Cassidy that it probably would be a long time before I had the pleasure of eating more of her swell fried cakes, as I was headed for Oak Island with three of my chums, who were as hungry as I was, to start living in a cave.

"Laws-a-me!" cried the old lady in a shrill voice, stabbing at the sizzling fried cakes with a long-handled fork. " 'Tis with envy that I listen to ye, Jerry. Fur all me life, outdoor lover that I am, I've wanted to live in a cave." Her wig falling over her eyes, she angrily yanked it off. "Drat the pesky thing," she kicked it into a corner. "I don't mind it in winter, fur it helps to keep me ould head warm.

But 'tis nothin' short of an abomination in summer.''

Asked then if Mr. Andrew Cadman had given us permission to use the canal island, I explained to her, as I filled my plate a second time, that the property now belonged to Mr. Randall Cliffe, Sr., a St. Louis millionaire, who planned later on to build a costly summer home there.

"Sure," she grinned, when I further explained that Mr. Cliffe, a boyhood chum of Dad's, had practically given us complete possession of the island until he got ready to build, " 'tis a big bug, ye are, hobnobbing with millionaires.''

"Mr. Cliffe is a nice man," I told her earnestly.

" 'Tis a big surprise to me," said she, "that Andrew Cadman ever sold the property. Fur I was told by Mrs. Morrison, queer ould woman that she was, that the island, which she inherited from her father, was the *one* piece of property that she wouldn't put a price on. She had a reason, she said, with an air of mystery, fur keepin' it in the family.''

I inquired curiously who Mrs. Morrison was.

"An' have ye never heard of *her?*" I was given a look of surprise. "Laws-a-me! When ye told me about the island changin' hands I took it fur granted that ye knew who the former owners were, down through Nicholas Barr and his daughter, to Andrew Cadman. Mrs. Morrison, the daughter, is the ould lady who put up her own tombstone in the Ashton cemetery an' then accurately predicted her death. I was there, with others, the night she died. An' niver will I furgit it. Fur we all knew how she believed in spooks. 'Twas somethin' she picked up while on a trip to Haiti. Voodooism! That's what some people call it. 'Tis a queer mess. I don't pretend to understand it. But a big change there was in Mrs. Morrison when she come home. An' then to have her predict her own death . . . an', mind ye, the clock stopped, too. Is it any wonder we were scared out of our wits? They tell me that Andrew Cadman never started the clock ag'in. An' to-day her room is just as it was when they carried her out in her coffin, nigh onto six years ago. There was a will. I don't remember the particulars. But Andrew Cadman got everything, an' him, mind ye, nothin' more than a common farm hand. Not even a distant relative. There was undue influence— him livin' with her that way, an' the two of 'em sharin' that crazy belief. I said so at the time; and I say so ag'in. Still,'' the old lady kind of checked herself, "I wouldn't want ye to repeat this, Jerry, fur 'tis no proof that I have. But to my notion the man, with his furtive eyes, shows what he is. . . . So he got twenty thousand dollars fur the island, ye say. The ould miser. An' did he show no hesitation about sellin' the land?"

"Not that I know of."

"Queer," she shook her bald head. "I can't git over the feelin' that he's actin' contrary to ould Mrs. Morrison's wishes. An' if he is— God pity his wretched soul. Fur she'll reach out of the grave an' drag him in. She *said* that she could come back in spirit. An' I believe it. So, if we wake up some mornin' an' find him strangled in his bed, we'll know who did it. *Voodooism!* What is it? I'd like to know. Yet, in a way, I'd be afraid to know. Fur, as I say, it put a queer stamp on Mrs. Morrison—a stamp that she carried to her dying hour. Ough!" the old lady shivered. "The thought of it gives me the creeps. Let's quit talkin' about it."

Gee! She wasn't the only one who had the creeps. Would Mrs. Morrison get sore, and try to strangle us, if she saw us running around her mysterious island in cat-skin pants?

I wondered.

CHAPTER II

HIDDEN EYES

As written down in the preceding book of this series, the big cavern that we had tapped on Oak Island while searching for Professor Clatterby's vanished lizard, the ten-thousand-dollar *Heloderma,* had been named "Whispering Cave," for reasons given, and the old hand-hewn cave, which was a sort of anteroom to the new one, had been named "Bible Cave."

Which, I think, was the right idea. For, as you probably will recall, it was there, in the outer cave, the building of which is credited to a hermit, now dead, that I met the old Bible peddler. That was the time he caught me hiding under his bed. Gee! I'll never forget *him.* He sure was funny. It puzzled me to understand why a man in his business should be living in a hidden cave on a lonely canal island. In telling me his story he called himself a "gentleman of the cloth," which was just another way of reminding me throughout the long-winded recital, which dealt mostly with cannibals and "sleeping toes," that he was a minister.

But that was all a lie. Swindler that he was, instead, he properly wound up in the Steam Corners jail, from which he later escaped, as crazy as a loon, only to be run down again by the law and then locked up more securely than ever.

Several months have passed since the publication of the "Whispering Cave" book containing the complete story of the Rev. Joshua Jonathan Jacobs and his crooked Bible scheme. However, you mustn't get the idea from this lapse of time that the same number of months have passed since our triumphant return from Oak Island.

As a matter of fact, we hadn't been away from the island more than a week, having come home to sell our wild honey. That job completed, we now were hurrying back to the scene of our earlier adventures to raise our old scow, which, as you know, had sunk to the bottom, off the island's south shore, during a terrific summer storm. Furthermore, we were eager to complete the exploration of our new cave, regarding which we had pledged our parents to secrecy.

Having helped to expose the crooked Bible peddler, it was the general belief of our parents that the law, in time, would pay us a nice reward. For the old man had over four thousand dollars in his hidden money box. Once we actually had the money in our hands. Imagine that! But we let it get away from us, dumbbells that we were, through listening to Scoop's advice. He's all right. As a rule he makes a good leader. But he sure blundered that time. Not that we could have spent the money without getting the law's permission. But, as Dad said, possession of it would have helped our case. For if it turned out that the crazy prisoner had no relatives; and if it further turned out that considerable money was left over after the swindle had been made good, naturally the balance, whatever it was, would go to the finders.

Peg had seen the sheriff put the handcuffs on the swindler during the final arrest. And it was our big chum's story that the Steam Corners officer had further taken possession of the money box. So, having let the money slip through our fingers, all we could do now, as I say, was to wait hopefully on the law.

As further written down in the conclusion of the preceding volume, it had been our intention to tell the public about the new cave, charging admission. But now, in hurrying back to the island, after a week's absence, we had other plans. Instead of broadcasting the discovery of the new cave, one of the largest in the county, thereby attracting hundreds of curious people to the island, we intended to live in the cave, like Robinson Crusoe. Mr. Cliffe, who owned the island, didn't like the idea of turning it into a show place. We were welcome to use it, he said. But he didn't want the public there. For if anybody got lost in the big cavern, or hurt, he probably would have a heavy damage suit on his hands.

Oak Island, as I have mentioned before, particularly in the two books, JERRY TODD AND THE OAK ISLAND TREASURE, and JERRY TODD IN THE WHISPERING CAVE, is situated in a wide waters, of the same name, fourteen miles east of Tutter, between Ashton, our county seat, and the smaller town of Steam Corners.

To make every point of my story clear, I probably should explain that a canal "wide waters" is a place where boats meet and pass. Like a railroad siding. We have a small wide waters below Tutter, and there is another one between our town and Ashton, ten miles east of us. The big wide waters that I'm writing about in my story is a sort of lake, more than a mile wide and half again as long. The island, itself, high and rocky at the east end, with heavily wooded slopes ending in a cat-tail marsh at the west end, is situated to the north of the channel, which, running east and west, is marked off with parallel rows of piles driven into the mud.

Dad says that before the canal was built, years and years ago, the Oak Island wide waters was a swamp, a fine place according to report for wild ducks, and the island that I'm going to tell you about was a rocky knoll. Of its many trees the largest is an oak, growing on the highest point, and it is this outstanding oak that gained for the island its name.

In sea stories you read about ships stopping at islands, charted and otherwise, to replenish their water casks. But none of the barges passing through our canal ever stop for water at Oak Island, though the spring on the north shore, among the rocks, is widely known. As a matter of fact, the wide waters, outside of the channel, is very shallow. And a canal boat couldn't land on the island even if its commander so desired. The piles that I have mentioned were put there to warn navigators of the dangerously shallow water beyond. It was one of these sunken piles that wrecked our scow, ripping a hole in the plank bottom, after which, as could be expected, the faithful old boat, with its home-made power plant and happy memories, had sunk to the bottom, in about three feet of water.

One of the island's first owners, as mentioned by Mrs. Cassidy, was a tavern keeper by the name of Nicholas Barr. I had heard of him through Mr. Cliffe, for it was in the old tavern, now a ruin, that we planned to put up, in camping style, until we got our raft built, which explains why we had decided this trip to drive to the wide waters, though, as you know, on all other occasions we had made the trip by water. In addition to the island, Mr. Cliffe had bought the adjacent shore land on which the tavern stood, in order to get a right of way to the county highway, it being the millionaire's intended scheme to build a fancy bridge from the island to the north shore. As the old tavern was to be completely torn down, to make way for the proposed private road, we had the new owner's permission to use as much of the lumber (for our raft) as we needed. It was of no use to him, he said.

So, in addition to Mr. Meyers' chest of carpenter tools we had brought along an axe and a wrecking bar. We had nails, too. As Scoop said, in planning things, it would be fun building the raft, launching it from the north shore of the wide waters. Working from this raft, with the other tools that we had brought along for the purpose, we hoped to quickly raise the old scow, putting it in shape for further exciting use, after which the raft was to be broken up and made into a palisade, a good thing to have in front of our cave, we all agreed, as there was no telling when the neighboring cannibals might swoop down on us in their painted war canoes and attack us.

We never had given any thought to how Mr. Andrew Cadman had come into possession of the island. In fact, we knew little about him except, as the island's seller, he lived not far from the wide waters on a farm. Land frequently changes hands. So, to us there was nothing surprising in the fact that a man named Cadman was now selling land formerly owned by a pioneer named Barr. But, as written down, it was Mrs. Cassidy's story, as told to me in her kitchen, that Mr. Cadman, now a man of more than sixty years of age, had inherited the property from the old tavern keeper's daughter, an old woman herself at the time of her death, whose married name, I had been told, was Morrison.

Mrs. Cassidy's story further suggested queer things; even possible crooked work. But that was nothing to us. For we had Mr. Cliffe's permission to use the island. And even if Mrs. Morrison didn't want us there, for peculiar unknown reasons, she couldn't do anything about it. For she was dead.

Getting over my scare, as I ate some more fried cakes, I kind of laughed to myself over Mrs. Cassidy's crazy belief that the dead woman was liable to come back from the grave and put on a strangling party. That sounded shivery. But there was nothing in it. I guess, though, that I wouldn't have laughed quite so freely if I had known of the weird things that were going to happen to us.

Voodooism! Do you know what it is? Well, according to what we picked up later on in the way of information, it's a sort of sorcery, or witchcraft. A "voodooer" can kill people by putting a "spell" on them. That sounds crazy. But, strangely, scientists admit the truth of it. Given a lock of hair, a finger- or toe-nail, or a scrap of skin, the "voodooer" can do things, by working with this *netik,* that will cast a spell over the owner, eventually killing him. Doctors are of no help. Either the "voodooer" must be bought off or killed. That, in part, is what voodooism is. Mrs. Morrison had been attracted to the queer religion, if you wish to call it that, because of her belief in "spiritualism." That is why she was so sure, though dead, that she would be able to come back in "spirit."

Mrs. Dexter came into the kitchen to inquire, in her nice way, if I was getting plenty of fried cakes.

"Just see my new plate, Mother. Isn't it a beauty?"

I could tell by the way Mrs. Cassidy looked at the plate that she didn't think any more of it than I did.

"An' how much did ye pay fur *that?*" the old lady wanted to know.

Mrs. Dexter laughed.

"You'll scold me when I tell you."

"I had better ones to start housekeepin' with, poor as we were. . . . Tin dollars?"

"Mother, don't be ridiculous. This is a genuine Wedgwood, almost two hundred years old. *Ten* dollars! The very idea."

"Two hundred years old, ye say," the old lady kind of turned up her nose. "Sure, it looks it. . . . Twinty dollars?"

"I think I was lucky to get it for a thousand dollars. For, so far as I know, or anybody else with whom I have talked, it's the only Wedgwood of its kind in existence."

Gee! Imagine anybody paying a thousand dollars for a plate. And an old plate, at that. Mrs. Cassidy almost fell into the fried-cake kettle.

" 'Tis a sinful waste of money," the old lady

cried shrilly. "As I've told ye before, Mary
Ellen Dexter, the day's comin' when ye'll be
sorry fur your wanton extravagance. A thousand dollars fur *that!*" the word was empha-
sized scornfully. "I wouldn't give ye tin cints
fur it. Did ye ever hear of such brainless
folderol, Jerry?"

"Mother doesn't realize," Mrs. Dexter then
told me laughingly, "that I am not the only
dish lover in the world. Every piece that I
buy, however big the price may seem to be, is
an investment. Take this plate. The right
party will gladly pay me fifteen hundred dollars for it, should I ever care to part with it.
And the same is true, in proportion, of every
rare dish in my collection."

Later I went to the barn, having gotten Mrs.
Cassidy's permission to look around for a suitable strap. Entering the old building, little
used nowadays, I noticed that the outside upper
haymow door was open. Yet, when I came
from the barn two or three minutes later, this
same door, as it faced the back of the house,
was closed.

Could it be, I wondered, in growing excitement, putting my detective talents to work, that
some one was hiding in the haymow, secretly
watching the house? I thought of the thousand
dollar plate. Certainly, was my conclusion,

there was plenty of stuff here to attract a burglar.

Tiptoeing into the barn, I listened with sharpened ears at the foot of the ladder. But there was no sound. Getting up courage, I cautiously climbed the ladder, finding the haymow empty.

And the door that had been closed so mysteriously was now hooked on the inside.

I needed no further proof than this of hidden eyes. And running breathlessly to the back door I told Mrs. Dexter of my suspicions. But instead of being alarmed, like me, she just laughed in her care-free way. The neighbor boys very often played in her barn, she said.

Which was true enough. But, even so, this didn't look to me like boys' work. And I told her so.

"Well, Jerry," her eyes twinkled, "if you're dead sure, as a Juvenile Jupiter Detective, that a mysterious burglar is scheming to molest my collection, I'll promise to keep a revolver under my pillow to-night. Furthermore, I'll make it a point to see that the doors and windows are all securely bolted."

When the harness was fixed, and we were on our way again, hoping that Mrs. Dexter would forgive us for the accident to her pansy bed,

I told the others about the hidden eyes in the haymow.

Red flopped the lines.

"Let's hurry and get away."

"Why?" grinned Scoop, who understands the freckled one like an open book.

"*Why?* Say, you give me a pain."

Scoop is a monkey.

"I yearn to go back," he got up and made a big gesture, shoving out his arms in the direction of the old-fashioned house, fast disappearing behind us. "In fact, as a Juvenile Jupiter Detective, I feel that it is my duty to go back. What do you say, fellow sleuths?"

Which, of course, was all done for Red's benefit.

"Shut up!" screeched the freckled driver. "We aren't going back. Do you hear that? I've had enough of your blamed old detective stuff. This is a vacation. And for once in my life I'm going to have fun without getting mixed up in something spooky."

Gee! And to think of what happened.

CHAPTER III

THE TAVERN IN THE FOREST

THE fun we had that hot summer's afternoon! I'll never forget it as long as I live. Peg, the big monkey, got out and straddled the horse's back, like a circus performer. Then we stopped beside the road and decorated our "chariot" with dandelions and other truck. We even hung a wreath on old Chris. People meeting and passing us in the dusty country road, as it wound in the general direction of Steam Corners, stared at us as though they thought we had escaped from the county crazy house. But that was all right. We expected it. If they hadn't looked at us that way we would have been disappointed. It was part of the fun.

For a change we colored our faces with red clay, dropped by a passing brickyard clay truck, pretending that we were Indians. Boy, you should have heard our peachy war whoops. We had different kinds. Sometimes we yelled in turn; other times we yelled in pairs, one pair trying to out-yell the other; but the best of all was when we yelled together.

As old Chris seemed unwilling to travel faster than a dogtrot, it was easy for us to jump out and in as the surrey jogged along. We played "street-car conductor," with Scoop hanging to the sides, collecting fares, and me banging a frying pan to clear the traffic. Once our cat box came loose, falling on two of the dogs. Gee! You never heard so much yowling and growling in all your life. We found out then that by singing real loud we could make the cats yowl beautifully. So, after that, in meeting people, instead of giving war whoops, we sang to beat the cats. And the harder we sang the harder the cats yowled. Regular grand-opera stuff.

Pretending that he was an ape, like in the "Tarzan" books, Peg climbed into the trees beside the road, making faces at us, with his long black hair pulled down over his eyes. When he was in the very top of one of the tallest trees we drove off and left him. But he soon overtook us. And what do you know, strong ox that he is, if he didn't grab one of the hind wheels of our "chariot" and dump us all into the roadside ditch. That is the way we kept it up all the afternoon—first one crazy stunt and then another. Talk about *fun*. As I say, it's something I'll remember all my life.

A finer day for such a trip couldn't be imag-

ined. The birds, as they fluttered in and out
of the trees and bushes, sang to us at the top
of their voices, to let us know, I guess, how
glad they were that we had come to live with
them. We could see honeybees and big yellow
bumblebees at work in the clover patches beside the road. Once, while we were singing, a
grasshopper flew into Scoop's face and he almost swallowed it—meaning the grasshopper,
of course, and not his face. Everywhere there
was a pleasing summery drone in the sultry
air. As I say, it sure was bully. A trip of this
kind, into the open, always puts pep into a
fellow. And how much more fun it is when the
day is just right!

Our road took us around Ashton, to the
north, so all we saw of the county seat was a
hazy outline of distant church steeples smothered in factory smoke. Shortly before five
o'clock old Chris of his own accord turned to
the right into a "blind" road, which, I probably should explain, was the private road leading to Mr. Cadman's farmhouse, past the old
deserted tavern. A sign, posted at the entrance
to the private road, warned people to "keep
out." But, as Scoop said, grinning, we didn't
believe in signs. And did we ever brag on our
nice horse. More than being smart, he was a
mind reader, we agreed.

Circling to the top of a wooded knoll, we got our first return view of the wide waters. And there in the middle of the big lake, as we sometimes called the wide waters, was our island. *Our* island, mind you. Oh, gee! I can't begin to describe the happy feeling that stole over me. It was, in fact, something more than mere happiness—a sort of reverent thankfulness, I guess. God gives boys life and health, which is proof of His great love for them. But just think of all the extra things that had been given to us—an island, thirteen cats, seven dogs and a boiled ham. Yes, sir, we sure were lucky.

The island and its surrounding lake having disappeared from our sight on our way down the hill, which, from the appearance of the rutted wheel tracks, seemed to be a mammoth gravel knoll, probably piled up by an early glacier, we found ourselves, in growing wonderment, in a dense forest. Such big trees were unusual for Illinois, for the most of our standing timber, according to report, is "second growth," the original big trees having been cut off by the early pioneers. But here was a forest, seemingly covering hundreds of acres, that had been protected.

The farther we entered the forest the denser it got. Which, of course, was perfectly all right with us. For, as Scoop said, being pioneers, ourselves, the wilder the scenery the better.

Then, in the very heart of the forest, in a clearing now grown up to weeds and underbrush, we came upon the old tumble-down tavern, over the front door of which, to our surprise, still hung the swinging sign that its early builder had put there. Warped with age, its iron support and metal trimmings coated with rust, the lettering of the sign, nevertheless, stood out bright and clear. As the name of the tavern has an important bearing on my story, I'll draw a picture of the sign as we first saw it. Here it is:

From the interesting sign, which we could not doubt had been touched up recently with fresh paint, we turned our attention to the old wooden building, itself, the doors and windows of which had long ago been carried away. At one time, no doubt, an attempt had been made by the owners to keep the openings boarded up, but even these rough blinds, where they hadn't fallen into decay, had been torn loose. So we had no difficulty gaining admittance, finding in the first room that we visited, evidently a sort of living room, that the floor, in one corner, was entirely rotted away. Below us was a deep, black hole, apparently without windows. It seemed more like a dungeon than a cellar. One look was enough for me. Br-r-r-r! A fine place, I told the others, turning away, for snakes and toads.

We counted seven lower rooms, three of which, judging from their small size, had been bedrooms. Everywhere we went the shaky floor was littered with fallen plaster and other rubbish. With that black hole underneath, and more loose stuff overhead, I didn't feel any too safe, I want to tell you.

There was a huge yawning fireplace in the living room, opposite which we saw a sagging, railless stairs leading to the upper rooms. It would be a big surprise to us, Red said, acting kind of scared, as usual, if we went upstairs and found a bear. But much less than being attacked by a wild animal, we found nothing but empty rooms, where, as below, the uneven floor was littered with stuff.

There was an attic. But we had no convenient way of reaching the closed trapdoor in the upper hall ceiling. And rather than monkey around in further exploration, which was largely a waste of time, anyway, we decided to get set for the night, realizing that the darkness would come early, shut in, as we were, by the dense forest.

So, unhitching patient old Chris, and turning him loose to forage for his own supper, we lugged our stuff into the house, tying the dogs to a ring in the wall at the foot of the stairs. Then, in good housekeeping style, we rigged up a broom and swept the living-room floor, after which we built a roaring fire in the old fireplace, Scoop having earlier pronounced the chimney safe.

Peg got supper while Red carried wood, it having been agreed that we were to work in pairs. In the meantime Scoop and I set out for the wide waters, a short distance away, where we found a water-logged skiff, in which, at the risk of getting a ducking, we later paddled to the island for drinking water, there being no sign of a well near the tavern.

Boy, this was the life. And did "hot-dogs"

ever taste so good to us as they did that night, roasted to perfection in the old fireplace, to feed the flames of which Red had gathered enough wood, picked up here and there, to last for a week. In addition to the "hot-dogs," we had canned beans, warmed up, and tomato soup. A feast fit for a king, I'll tell the world. We should have had cocoa, too, but when Peg came to pour it out he found a big green spider in it, so no one would drink it.

The cats and dogs each got a "weenie" apiece and some other truck, which, as you can imagine, made a big hole in our food supply. So we decided to take them over to the island the first thing in the morning, where they were to be turned loose to shift for themselves. They could eat toads and things like that, Scoop said. Or, for a change, we could put out bull-head lines and fill them up on fish. Moreover, there were plenty of turtles waiting to be caught.

When supper was over we put our stuff away, in proper camping style, and having taken care of the dogs and cats, as mentioned, we went outside to see how old Chris was faring. He looked hungry. So, wanting to do the right thing by him, we ran here and there, gathering handfuls of clover. Then we took him to the canal and watered him, after which, to his further comfort, we pulled weeds and made him a nice soft bed on the canal bank. This was better, we figured, than taking him into the old tavern with us where he was liable to fall through the rotten floor and break his neck. Nor was there room for him in the old shed where we had put our surrey.

At Peg's suggestion we stripped and played water tag, which was fun. But we cheerfully turned the canal over to the croaking frogs and hungry mosquitoes when the sun went down, after which, hurrying back to the tavern, we heaped fresh fuel on our fire, thus driving out the queer black shadows that had crept into the old building to hide in the corners.

Gathered around the roaring fire, we fell to talking about the probable early history of the old tavern, which, we understood, had been liberally patronized by drovers and grain haulers, there being no railroads or canal boats in those early days. It was hard for us to imagine loaded grain wagons passing over the rutted road that we had followed in coming here, but probably that was the only kind of roads that the early farmers had known.

The moon came up shortly after nine o'clock. But its light made no impression on the blackness of the surrounding forest. Stretched out in the glow of the fire, at peace with the world and all that was in it, we felt no particular alarm when something with a pair of green eyes came to the door of our "castle," giving us the curious "once over." The dogs set up a fearful racket, scaring the animal away, though later we fancied we heard it prowling around on the other side of the house.

But what did scare us, in a way, particularly Red, was the crazy ghost story that Scoop made up about the old tavern keeper, in whose deep, dank cellar, we were told, countless secret graves had been dug at the mystic hour of midnight, that being the villainous proprietor's customary way of disposing of the chilled bodies of his murdered victims.

"Oh, gee," said Red, with big eyes. "You never heard that anybody really was murdered here, did you?"

"Absolutely," nodded Scoop, nudging me on the sly. Then he held up his hands for silence. "Sh-h-h-h!" said he mysteriously, looking toward the yawning hole in the floor.

"What was it?" Red inquired.

"Sounded to *me* like bones rattling," Peg put in, to help the fun along.

But Red isn't wholly dumb.

"Aw, you shut up," he yelled at the big one, in sudden anger. "You're just trying hard to scare me."

He got up then to put some fresh fuel on the fire, which had burned away to a bed of red coals. And noticing that he was acting queer,

I searched his face, finding it as white as chalk.

"Look!" he cried, pointing to one of the windows.

To tell the truth, crazy as it may seem to you, I actually expected to see a ghost. The freckled one's actions suggested it. And for a moment or two I was scared out of my wits. But there was nothing in the window so far as I myself could see.

"It was a man," the frightened one then told us. "I saw his face. It was a mean face, too. And he was watching us."

Peg knows no fear. So it didn't surprise us when he ran outside. But the mysterious prowler had vanished into the night. Nor were the dogs able to pick up his scent when we turned them loose. Much less than helping us, two of them ran off, which was the last we ever saw of them.

A rusted dirk, thrust into the wooden window sill, held a note. Here it is:

There's a worse peril in this house than ghosts. So take warning and save your lives while you've got the chance.

(*Signed*)

The true owner of
the King's Silver.

CHAPTER IV

DETECTIVE WORK

A "PERIL" worse than ghosts! Standing in the moonlight, in front of the tavern, Peg holding the rusted dirk and Scoop the mysterious note, which, as you can imagine, had left us with a queer feeling in our backbones, we stared apprehensively at the weather-beaten old building, half expecting, I guess, to have some hideous, unearthly monster lunge, screaming, through an open window.

Yet, in a way, though frightened, as I say, I wasn't particularly surprised. For it has been my experience, as written down in the various books to my credit, that most old buildings have queer secrets. Usually it's a "ghost." Yet, in this case, if we were to believe the strange note, a "peril," worse than "ghosts," was hanging over us.

What could it be?

The note, in itself, wasn't a threat. It didn't order us to vacate. It simply warned us to leave, with whole skins, as you might say, while we had a chance.

Yet, the manner in which the note had been

pinned to the window sill, with the rusted dirk, which in itself suggested bygone, reckless days, left little doubt in our minds of what was liable to happen to us if we failed to heed the grim warning.

Throughout Scoop's crazy ghost story the dogs had stirred restlessly. We had noticed it. And now we knew that a fifth pair of ears had been tuned in on the story. The writer's mention of "ghosts" proved that he had overheard us. And while we hadn't suspected his presence under the window, the dogs, due to their peculiar senses, had smelt him, which, as I say, accounted for their restlessness.

Plainly, the note had not been written by Andrew Cadman, whose lonely farmhouse, we had been told, was situated farther east, beyond the forest. For the farmer, if he had wanted to get rid of us, would have walked in on us without ceremony, curtly ordering us out. The note was signed: "The true owner of the King's Silver." Mr. Cliffe, supposedly, was the new owner of the property. Yet, here was some one of unknown identity who openly claimed to be the *true* owner. And whoever this owner was, he had a reason, to his own hidden interests, or possibly to ours, for wanting to get rid of us.

Well, it was very evident that he didn't know

the truth about us. He thought that we were just four ordinary kids on a camping trip. As a matter of fact, as has been mentioned, we were four Juvenile Jupiter Detectives on a vacation—only the indications were that it was liable to be a much more exciting "vacation" than any of us had suspected.

"Oh, gee," suffered Red, spreading his gab around as usual. "I never expected anything like *this*. Shall we pack up and go home?"

He knew, of course, that none of us would want to go home. But, as I say, it's his nature to blat around that way, pretending that he's scared to death. As a matter of fact, deep down in his heart, he was fully as eager as we were to stay and solve the mystery.

That is what *any* detective would have done.

A good plan, we decided, would be to pack up, with every appearance of being scared out of our wits, and supposedly start for home. Believing us gone for good, the "true" owner of the King's Silver, as he styled himself, would then return. So, to spot him, in clever detective style, all we had to do was to come back to the clearing on the sly.

Not, however, that we had any right to nab him, or anything like that. But, as detectives, we were curious to learn who he was. There was a mystery here, and we wanted to solve it.

"Who's going to harness the horse?" said Peg, when we were ready to leave.

"Let Red do it," said Scoop.

"*Me?*" piped up cold feet. "Go tie a knot in a noodle."

"It's your horse," argued Scoop. "You picked it out."

"You can have it," Red broke out with sudden generosity.

"But why bother with the horse?" I put in, realizing that they were just talking to make a noise, it having been earlier decided that old Chris was to be left where he was. "I'd rather start out afoot," I added.

"*What?*" soloed Peg at the top of his voice. "And desert the cats?"

"This is no time to think of cats," I told him. "Forget about the cats."

The dogs seemed to know what was going on. For when we started out single file, Peg leading, they set up a fearful racket, wanting, of course, to be taken along. Then, to swell the chorus, the cats tuned in. But a detective can't be bothered with cats and dogs, so we went on without them. As Scoop said, we might see them again and we might not. But it was nothing to worry about. For even if the "true" owner did turn them loose, there were other dogs and cats to be had.

The moon tried hard to peek at us through

the trees, but with little success. And having come to the edge of the forest, after a walk of probably fifteen minutes, we hid our stuff in the weeds, marking the spot, after which we left the main track and started back through the forest, the leader having told us to separate. But Red wouldn't hear to such a thing. So he and I kept together, or, rather, he hung to me as though I were some kind of a life saver.

" 'The King's Silver,' " said he, sort of reflective-like. "That's an odd name for a tavern. Don't you think so, Jerry?"

"All old taverns have odd names," I told him, hurrying along.

"But what does it mean?"

"It's just a name," I said. "Probably it doesn't mean anything at all."

"I bet it does," he hung on.

"Well, then, if you know so much about it," I grunted, "why come to me for information?"

"We don't have any kings in this country," was his further reflective remark.

"What of it?"

"I was just thinking that 'The King's Silver' would be a swell name for a tavern in England, where they have a king. But in this country it ought to be 'The President's Tavern,' or 'George Washington's Tavern.' Don't you think so?"

"Nicholas Barr was an Englishman," I told

him, remembering what I had heard about the old innkeeper. "So that may explain why he called his tavern 'The King's Silver.' "

"We aren't far from the county cuckoo house, Jerry."

"*You* ought to know," I grinned.

"Maybe," he added, "one of the nuts connected up with an open window."

I saw what he meant.

"Some one who imagines that he's Nicholas Barr, huh?"

"Why not?"

"I hope you're wrong," I told him, after a moment's reflection. Certainly, I had no desire to mix up with an escaped crazy man.

Scoop and Peg were waiting for us at the edge of the clearing, the leader holding a sheet.

"It's mine," Red promptly identified the sheet in the moonlight. "Where'd you get it?"

"Peg picked it up."

"I must have lost it."

"You'd lose your head if it wasn't fastened to you."

Which was true, all right, though Red was in no mood to admit it.

"If I did lose my head," was his return shot, "I surely wouldn't get much if I got yours."

At the leader's further orders we then crawled through the weeds, coming at length to a favorable spot within thirty feet of the main door. And here we lay flat, in complete silence.

A familiar whinny came from the direction of the canal.

"Old Chris," breathed Scoop.

Presently the old gray horse came into sight at the edge of the clearing. We thought that he had come to feed, but, instead, he went directly to the tavern, where he thrust his shaggy head through an open window, repeating the mournful whinny that had first drawn our attention to him.

"He's looking for us," Scoop breathed again.

It's a good thing that we didn't show ourselves. For suddenly some one came into sight around the corner of the tavern.

"The crazy man," I breathed in Red's ear.

But on second glance I saw, in growing wonderment, that it was a boy.

And Red had insisted that the "prowler" was a man!

"You're good," Peg told the freckled one, who, for once in his life, had nothing to say in return.

Well, as you can imagine, it was a big surprise to all of us to learn that the "true" owner was a boy. And the meeting between the strange kid and the old horse was still another surprise.

"Why, Christopher," came to us in a pleased

voice. "I never expected to see *you* again.
Good old Christopher! Were you lost in the
woods? Unable to find you, I made up my mind
that the gypsy had stolen you."

Boy, as Scoop said, this was getting more
complicated every minute. If the old horse had
indeed been stolen, it would seem that we un-
knowingly had brought it back to the very place
where it belonged.

A stolen horse! No wonder Red had gotten
such a big bargain.

The dogs were barking. But they quieted
down when the newcomer went inside. Creep-
ing closer, we saw him petting them.

"Five dogs," he spoke to himself. "And
look at the *cats*. Gee-miny crickets! Those
boys surely must like cats. Queer, too, that
they should go off and leave them."

There was a mystery about this boy. We
realized that, all right. Otherwise, he wouldn't
be hiding in a place like this. He probably had
a secret reason, too, we figured, for repainting
the old sign and calling himself the "true"
owner of the King's Silver.

Climbing the stairs he disappeared from our
sight, after which we could hear him doing
something in the upper hall. It was Peg who
hit the nail on the head. The stranger, old
hefty said, in good guesswork, was monkeying
around under the attic trapdoor.

What the kid actually did, as we learned later on, was to push up the trapdoor with a stick, after which he pulled down a rope ladder which was kept there for that purpose, he having made the ladder himself.

He later came downstairs with a roll of bedding, which was spread out in front of the fireplace. And taking note of the red coals he built up the fire, after which he rolled himself in his blankets for the night.

Which proved, the leader said, that the story of the "peril" was a myth. The kid had worked us, with the made-up story, in order to get rid of us.

What he needed, Scoop declared, was a dose of his own medicine. So, getting the sheet that Red had dropped, the leader had us fasten it on him, in regular "ghost" style, with big black circles for eyes, after which he "glided" into the tavern, groaning and grinding his teeth.

And now comes the funny part!

Instead of being scared, the kid tackled the "ghost," football fashion, the latter going down in a heap. And when we got there Scoop was yelling bloody murder.

Gee! Could that kid ever scrap! He was a regular fury. I honestly believe that the black hair stood up all over his head.

"Hey!" squawked Scoop. "Let me up. What do you think I am?—a punching-bag?"

"You *will* try to scare me, huh?" socked the kid, with flashing eyes.

Scoop took his medicine with a grin.

"And now, Mr. King's Silver," he completely threw aside the sheet, when the other boy stepped back, suspicious of us, "let me introduce you to the rest of the gang. This noble-looking guy with the broad shoulders and dirty neck is Peg Shaw, our official heavy-weight. Knowing how well he can use his fists, I'm glad, for your sake, that *he* wasn't the 'ghost.' The handsome chap with the pug nose is Jerry Todd, our pet scribe. And this abbreviated summary of a freckle epidemic is Red Meyers."

Slowly the suspicion and distrust died out of the boy's face. Then, as we extended our hands, in real friendship, he grinned sheepishly. Returning our handclasp, he told us that his name was Alfred Moore.

"You fooled me," he admitted. "I thought that you had gone home."

"We intended to fool you," grinned Scoop.

"But weren't you afraid," came quizzically, "when you found my note?"

"Somewhat. But our detective curiosity outweighed our fears. We never dreamed, though, that you were a boy. And now that we know the truth, I sure am glad that we didn't skin out with cold feet."

"So am I," said the kid feelingly. And when he raised his eyes we saw that they were troubled.

Then, with no further hesitation, he told us his story. But as it is a rather long story, going back a great many years, I think I had better make it the subject of a new chapter.

CHAPTER V

WE first heaped the fireplace full of wood. And as the flames jumped up, with long red tongues, filling the room with puddles of light, a peculiar sadness took hold of the new boy. Staring silently into the blaze, his chin cupped in his hands, his thoughts plainly far away, he seemed to forget for the moment that we were there. Our curiosity grew. But eager as we were to hear his story, we said nothing to disturb him, content to let him take his own time and think things out in his own way.

Watching him, as he sat there in the dancing firelight, I was more impressed than ever by his very evident manliness. There was something about him—possibly it was the way he squared his shoulders when he spoke, or in the firm expression of his rugged face—that said as plainly as words that he knew how to take care of himself under any and all circumstances. Women, I suppose, giving particular attention to the length of his black eyelashes and the shape of his mouth, would have said that he was good-looking. But what meant more to us than his mere good looks was his grit. Boy, the way he had waded into Scoop!

It is by such gritty acts that a kid shows what he's made of. And Al, as we now called him, had amply proved to us that he was a pal worth having. Nor did we, for that matter, ever change our early opinion of him. If anything, in the days that followed, our admiration for him grew as we fought beside him, like regular pirates, to right the wrong that had been shoved on him by a greedy old man. Yes, sir, Al sure was the right sort. Fair and square all the way through. And as smart as he was gritty. Mindful of the tough time that he had as a boy, I'll always be glad that we had the chance to help him. He sure was deserving of everything that we did for him.

Realizing suddenly that our eyes were boring holes in him, sort of, he lifted his face from his hands and regarded us with equal curiosity.

"What did you think," he inquired, as a beginning, "when you saw the new sign over the tavern door?"

"We wondered at it," Scoop admitted.

"Yet you never suspected," the questioner continued his curious look at us, "that another boy was hiding here?"

"No," the leader shook his head.

"I walked to Ashton this afternoon, having,

as usual, hid my bedding and other stuff in the
attic. When I got back at eight o'clock imagine
my surprise to find a gang of four strange boys
in possession of the house! I didn't know what
to do. If I showed myself, claiming my stuff,
the newcomers would wonder who I was and
what my object was in hiding here. I had reasons for wanting to avoid their questions.
Moreover, there was no certainty that I
wouldn't get kicked out, as that is what a lone
boy often gets at the hands of a strange gang.''

''Not with this gang,'' Scoop spoke up in our
defense. ''We aren't that kind.''

''But there are such boys.''

''Sure thing,'' conceded Scoop, thinking of
the Stricker cousins, Bid and Jimmy. ''We
have such a gang in Tutter.''

''Not knowing who you were, I was afraid of
you. Certainly, I had no thought then of taking a gang of strange boys into my confidence.
So, with the hope of scaring you away, I wrote
the note that you found outside.''

''But where did you get the old dirk?'' Red
put in curiously, remembering how the note had
been pinned to the window sill.

''*That?* Oh, I dug it up.''

''Dug it up?'' repeated Red, staring at the
stranger with quickened interest. ''Then you
must have been looking for something.''

INSTEAD OF BEING SCARED, THE KID TACKLED THE "GHOST."
Jerry Todd Pirate.   *Page* 45

The boy nodded.

"Treasure?" Red followed up.

"Sure thing," came another nod.

The freckled one's eyes almost popped out of his head.

"Gee-miny crickets!" he cried. "Do you really mean it?"

"Haven't any of you boys ever heard about the lost silver?" the question was then put to us curiously, as we stared at one another in growing excitement.

Lost silver! And the tavern's name was *The King's Silver*. Plainly Red had hit the nail on the head in suspecting that the tavern's peculiar name had a hidden meaning.

To our further amazement the boy then told us that he was a great-grandson of the old tavern keeper, and also a grandson of Mrs. Morrison, the queer old lady who, so strangely, had accurately predicted her own death.

"My mother," the speaker then went deeper into his story, as we listened attentively, "ran away from home, marrying my father, John Moore, in Indiana, where I was born. My grandmother, having inherited the family property, was wealthy, but my father and mother had nothing. I'm almost ashamed to tell you how poor we were. There were times when we hadn't enough to eat. That was my father's

fault, for he kept jumping from one job to another. And much of the time he didn't work
at all.''

"We have a man like that in Tutter," Red
spoke up. "His real name is Bill Granger, but
everybody calls him Major Hoople, after the
lazy guy in the funny pictures."

Gee! That shows you how little Red knows.
The big dumb-bell. He hasn't any manners at
all. I felt like giving him a swift boot in the
seat of the pants.

The story-teller flushed.

"Yes," he admitted soberly, "my father *was*
lazy. I can't deny it. And that is why my
grandmother had forbidden the marriage. But,
as I say, my mother wasn't to be stopped.
Well, when I was eight years old my father
died. Before his death my mother wrote home,
begging forgiveness and asking for help.
Money was needed, she explained, to hire a
nurse and buy medicine. But the letter never
was answered. So, like my mother, who, in
bitterness, never wrote home again, I always
shall feel that my grandmother was partly re-
sponsible for my father's death. Oh," the boy
looked at us doggedly, "he wasn't all that a
father should be—I know that. But my mother
loved him, hard as her life was after she married him. And I loved him, too."

Again, as the past crowded in on his mind, the boy fell into silence, staring at the fire. And for a moment or two I held my breath, sort of, expecting old spotted nose to make another one of his dumb-bell cracks. But for a wonder he kept his mouth shut.

"My father's death left us poorer than ever," the story was resumed. "My mother struggled along, as best she could, trying to make a home for the two of us. But she wasn't strong. And the work that she had to do, bending over washboards and scrubbing people's floors on her hands and knees, killed her. I was ten then. The neighbors were good. I remember. They asked me if they should send for my grandmother. I told them *no.*"

"Atta-boy!" cried Peg. "I would have done the same, myself."

"It was a shabby funeral," the boy went on. "I'll always remember it—what a cold, drizzly day it was, and how I shivered. The neighbor women cried over me. Women are that way. Later, without telling me about it, the minister took it upon himself to write to my grandmother, explaining that I was all alone in the world. The letter was answered by a man named Andrew Cadman, who said that my grandmother, too, was dead. And instead of being rich, as most people supposed, it was doubtful, Cadman wrote, if the property would bring enough to pay the back taxes and other debts.''

Remembering what Mrs. Cassidy had told me about the schemer who had sold the island to Mr. Cliffe, I was filled with sudden excitement.

''Cadman lied to you,'' I cried. ''Your grandmother was a rich woman. Why, just the other day a piece of land that she owned sold for twenty thousand dollars. And this timber is worth another twenty thousand.''

''I know now,'' nodded the boy, ''that Cadman lied in his letter. I've learned a lot of things since coming here. This afternoon I had a lawyer look up my grandmother's queer will, which is on record in the Ashton courthouse. Evidently she felt that the will wasn't important. For Cadman was made 'custodian' of the estate until, as she expressed it, she was ready to come back, spiritually, to handle the estate, herself.''

That puzzled Scoop.

''But how could she come back,'' the leader spoke up, ''when she was dead?''

''She thought that she could come back,'' said the boy. ''That was her belief.''

''They call it spiritualism,'' I explained to the leader. ''Mrs. Cassidy told me all about it one day.''

"Bunk," said Scoop.

"According to what my mother told me," the boy then went on, "my grandmother was a very peculiar woman. It was her belief, as Jerry says, that she could come back from the grave in spirit form. So, instead of disposing of her property, she placed it in Cadman's hands, to be held in trust, subject to her further 'spiritual' orders. Can you imagine such a crazy thing? And what helped Cadman was a clause which stated that the property was to be his, in fact, if he received no 'spiritual' orders over a period of five years, or if no blood relative appeared in that time to claim the estate. Had I showed up within the five-year period, I could have inherited everything. Now it is too late. And it was to keep me away until the five years were up that Cadman lied to the minister."

"The dirty crook!" cried Red, with flashing eyes.

"But how about the lost silver?" Scoop put in. "Did Cadman get that on you, too?"

"Yes," cried Red, "tell us about the silver."

"After a few months," the boy went on, leading up to the part of the story that we were waiting for, "I was taken to the poorhouse. I didn't like it there. It was all old people. So I was glad when a man came along and took me to raise. I thought that I was going to get a good home. For the man talked nice. And so

did his wife. It was 'dearie' this and 'dearie'
that. But there was no 'dearie' business when
they got home. Benjamin Clud was a farmer.
And his only object in taking me out of the
poorhouse, I learned, was to get a chore boy,
or, rather, a family slave. He was too stingy
to hire a boy. He got *me* for nothing. Oh, I
got my meals . . . such as they were. I got
my clothes, too—a nice new pair of overalls
every six months! They had to keep me in
school. That was in the agreement. But I
heard about it—what a waste of time it was.
All they did was nag at me. I was there for
more than three years. And in all that time I
never had a suit of clothes. Mrs. Clud told
the neighbors that she didn't buy me a suit because I was growing so fast. Last winter I
didn't even have underwear. They thought
that they could keep me out of school by freez-
ing me. But I would have gone to school with
bare skin showing. For I realized that my only
chance to get a good job when I grew up was to
learn all I could.

"Last April Clud took me out of school to
help him plow. I thought that in a week or two
I would be back in school. But he had other
plans. He found that he could make some
extra money by hiring me out to his neighbors
when he didn't need me at home. So I went

from farm to farm, working like a nigger . . . and *he* got the money.

"I hated him for that. And I hated Mrs. Clud, too. They were two of a kind. She had the dirtiest house in the neighborhood. And her meals, as I say, matched her house. Can you imagine anybody being too stingy to eat? Well, *they* were. I always got up from the table hungry. Yet you should have heard the old hen bawl me out for gorging myself. And when I tried to keep clean, she hid the soap on me, telling me that I washed too often."

"Gee," said Red, with a comical look. "That isn't what my ma tells me."

"Well, to go on with my story, I made up my mind, a month ago, that the time had come to skin out. I was big enough to support myself. Certainly, I concluded, realizing that my school days were over, I couldn't be any worse off than where I was. Clud had papers that bound me to him until I was twenty-one, at which time he was under obligation to give me a team of horses, a hundred dollars in money, and a Bible. But I had no intention of letting the papers stop me from running away. I had had enough of old Clud. I hoped that I'd never see him again. And once I got safely away, I was determined to keep out of his sight until I was of age.

"My mind made up to run away, as I say, my first thought was to go to the city. But I decided against that. I would be better off, I reasoned, in the country. Then, overnight, a peculiar longing came to me to come here, though until then I always had said that I never wanted to see my grandmother's home, or anything else belonging to her. That's the way I felt toward her. My mother had told me about the old tavern. I had heard, too, about the lost silver. Having been hidden by my great-grandmother, the silver, my mother said, never had been found, though different members of the family had searched high and low for it. I still believed, of course, that my grandmother had died a poor woman, leaving nothing behind except debts. However, the silver, if I could find it—and the thought of finding it was exciting—would make me rich. I had a right to it. But for fear that the new owner of the land would take the silver away from me, in case I found it, I decided, if I ever got here, to do my searching on the sly."

"What kind of silver do you mean?" questioned Red. "Money?"

"No. Silver dishes."

"Dishes?" I repeated, my thoughts jumping to Mrs. Dexter. "Do you mean that your great-grandmother hid her silver dishes?"

The boy nodded.

"It was called the King's Silver."

"Why," cried Red, "that's the name of the tavern."

"Sure thing. It was from my great-grandmother's famous silver dishes that the tavern got its name. . . . And you never heard about the lost King's Silver?" the question was put curiously.

Scoop shook his head.

"We didn't even know the name of the tavern until we came here."

"My mother hunted for the lost silver when she was a girl, as did the other boys and girls in the neighborhood, thus proving that it was no family secret. So, when I found you here, I figured, of course, that you, too, in knowing the story of the silver, had come to try your luck."

"I have a hunch," grinned Scoop, "that we're going to try our luck. Eh, gang?"

"You tell 'em," cried Peg, with dancing eyes. "Buried treasure! Oh, baby! In starting out this afternoon I never dreamed that anything so wonderful as this was going to happen to us."

"According to the story that my mother passed along to me, the silver came from England. It was given to a great-great-aunt of mine by the king, himself, my aunt having saved his life when a war was going on. Hard pressed by the enemy, the king hid in her cupboard, where he knocked down a lot of her best dishes. The enemy never found him. After the war the king came back, riding a milk-white horse all trimmed up with gold and jewels, just like a fairy story. On a black horse was a basket of silver—plates, cups, saucers, platters and goblets—enough to set a table for twelve people. It was all solid silver, too, made for the king's own use. It was my aunt's reward, he said, for having saved his life, and made up for all the dishes that he had smashed in getting out of her cupboard.

"Because the silver had been the king's, a lot of dukes and lords came to buy it, offering my aunt a big price for it. But she wouldn't sell a single piece. Dying, she left the set to her oldest daughter. And when *she* died it was left to my great-grandmother Barr, who brought it to America. For years it was kept in this room, in a locked cabinet that my great-grandfather built for it. Then one night it came up missing. And everybody said that my great-grandmother Barr had hidden it to save it from being stolen by a peddler called the hunchback."

"Gee!" cried Red. "This gets exciting."

"The hunchback was a bad egg. His mind was as crooked as his back. He tramped about the country selling tinware, but a lot of people said he made a living stealing. It wasn't safe to have him around. No one trusted him. The night the silver disappeared he came to the tavern just as the sun was going down, finding my great-grandmother and my grandmother, then a small girl, all alone, my great-grandfather, the tavern keeper, having gone to Chicago with a drove of cattle. My great-grandmother had no doubt that the hunchback, with his evil eyes on the valuable silver, had been waiting for this chance to catch her alone. So she made up her mind to hide the silver. Letting on that she wasn't scared she brought the hunchback a cup of coffee, in which she had put a sleeping powder. Later, when he was asleep, she took the silver, eight or ten pieces at a time, and hid it outdoors. Early the next morning my great-grandfather came home from his trip, a day ahead of time. And when the hunchback learned, in waking up, that he had been tricked, he threatened to strangle my great-grandmother. Maybe it was the scare that made her sick. Anyway, she went to bed that morning with a fever in her head that made her say all kinds of crazy things. But she never told where the silver was hid. And in four days she was dead. Later they searched high and low for her diary, in which it was believed that she had written down the silver's hiding place. But the diary, like the silver, never was found."

"And you say it's a true story?" Red showed some doubt.

"Absolutely. I've spent two weeks searching for the treasure. But all I've found so far is the old dirk you asked me about, which I dug out of the cellar floor, and some old brass rings."

"Finger rings?" inquired Red.

"No. Big earrings. It's further told in our family that a brother of my great-grandfather's was a pirate. So it may be that these earrings belonged to him. And the dirk, too."

"Gee!" Red cried. "This *is* exciting."

That, Al said, practically concluded his story. In running away he had taken a favorite old horse, figuring that he had a right to it, according to the terms of the paper that Mr. Clud had signed. Riding horseback nights, and hiding days, he at length had arrived at his mother's old home, where, after repainting the old sign, for the fun of it, he had put in his time treasure hunting. Having noticed a gypsy hanging around the tavern, he later discovered that his horse had been stolen.

In explaining how the old gray horse had

fallen into our hands, Scoop further recited the
details of our proposed "Robinson Crusoe"
scheme, describing, in conclusion, the big cave
that we had discovered on Oak Island. We
talked big, he said, about raising cats and getting rich from selling fur. But that was all a
sort of game, the object of which was to make
it seem, in our minds, that we were real Robinson Crusoes.

"It was the island," the leader wound up,
"that Mr. Cadman sold for twenty thousand
dollars."

"Yes," I told Al, "and he sold it against
your grandmother's wishes, too."

"How do you know?" came the quick in-
quiry.

"An old lady who was acquainted with your
grandmother told me so."

Al's eyes grew big.

"Do you suppose," then came the exciting
theory, "that my grandmother wanted to keep
the island in the family because she suspected
that the silver was hidden there?"

"Why not?" cried Red.

"I've dug in the cellar, and all over the yard,
but I never thought of the island, though I've
been going there every day, in an old skiff, for
drinking water."

"It wasn't an island in your great-grandmother's day," I told him. "For the canal, which forms the island, was built later on."

"Nevertheless," said he, "if there's caves there, as you say, I bet anything that's where the silver is."

"Sure thing," cried Red.

We then gave Al our pledge to stand by him and help him in every way we could. It would be fun hunting for the silver. And if we found it, we'd help him sell it. For there was a rich woman in Tutter, we explained, who paid big prices for old dishes. And if there were a hundred pieces in the set it wasn't improbable, was our big talk, that he'd end up with a check for a hundred thousand dollars.

It was one o'clock before we turned in. And never will I forget the happy, contented feeling that stole over me as I lay there in the firelight, wrapped in my blanket, Red on one side of me and our dandy new chum on the other side.

It seemed to me that the most wonderful adventures that a boy could wish for lay ahead of us. A lonely island! Explorations! Rafts! Caves! Buried treasure!

But how different would have been my feelings had I known the truth about the face that Red had seen at the window!

CHAPTER VI

UNEXPECTED VISITORS

THERE were no "beauty naps" the following morning. We had work to do, Peg said, noisily routing us out at five bells. Gee! Having been up until one o'clock, as written down in the preceding chapter, it was hard for me to squeeze the sleep out of my eyes. But once I was up, and had a good stretch, I enjoyed it.

The camper who knows his p's and q's never lies abed in the morning. And very often, when we're out on a trip like this, we get up with the sun, having learned from experience that the early morning is the best part of the whole day. Somehow at five o'clock the summer air seems cleaner and fresher. Growing things, wet with dew, smell sweeter. The birds, fresh from their rest, like human beings, are livelier and happier.

But, as I say, however much a fellow loves to get up with the robins, to share their joy of a new day, as you might say, it's hard to crawl out on less than five hours' sleep.

"Come on, you sticky-eyed guys," boomed

Peg, starting for the canal. "The last one in is 'it' for water tag."

Already we could feel the heat of the sun, which seemed to grin at us as it climbed into the sky, to let us know that it intended to keep a friendly eye on us throughout our coming work. Camping isn't camping, to my notion, unless the sun shines. And this surely was the beginning of one of the bulliest camping days I ever had known.

The turtles, of which there were many thousands in the wide waters, of different sizes, wondered, I guess, what in time was going on. We could see them, a short distance away, stretching their curious necks at us, as we yelled and flopped around in the water. Evidently they weren't used to such a crazy racket.

Swimming down the shore, Peg discovered a clay bank, after which, of course, we made ourselves some clay "tights," little dreaming that before many hours had passed we would be putting the clay to a more practical use.

The forest, near the canal, was full of laden raspberry bushes. And while Scoop and I were getting breakfast, it being our turn to do the cooking, the others, under Al's leadership, put on a clever little berry hunt. Boy, that sure was one grand breakfast. Scoop is the king-pin coffee maker of the county. At home I don't

care much for coffee, nor do my parents encourage me to drink it. But it sure hits the
spot on a camping trip. We had toast, browned
just right, which took patience (yah, a certain
guy by the name of Jerry Todd made it!), eggs,
fried hard in bacon grease, and, as a sort of
dessert, the fresh raspberries, of which we had
more than two quarts.

Al had a lot of canned stuff in the attic.
And I wondered at this, having gotten the impression, from his story, that he had left home
without a cent. I further wondered at his
clothes, which, if anything, were better than
ours. Certainly, was my puzzled thought, the
neat outing suit that he wore contradicted his
story of the overalls.

"What little I have," he told us earnestly,
when all of his stuff had been brought downstairs and added to ours, "I owe to the generosity of the old neighbors who helped bury my
father and mother. I stopped there overnight,
wearing ragged overalls. And hearing my
story, one of the men gave me thirty dollars,
which was money, he told me, probably making
up the story, that he owed my father. Another
old neighbor bought me these clothes. Gee!
I sure was happy. For, as I told you last night,
I hadn't had any decent clothes in more than
three years. Overalls are all right. But it

hurts a boy's pride when he has to wear them all the time. Lots of times, at Clud's, I wanted to dress up, but couldn't."

"My ma makes me dress up every Sunday," said Red.

"A fellow should," nodded Al, in his serious way. "I would have gone to Sunday school regularly if I had had clothes to wear like the other boys. But I couldn't go in overalls."

"And didn't you ever go to any Sunday-school picnics?"

"No," Al said soberly.

"It's fun to go to Sunday-school picnics. For the ladies always bring lots of good things to eat. I like to go to parties, too. One time at a party Jerry and I ate a whole cream cake. Didn't we?" he stuck out his neck at me.

"You seem to know," I grunted, disgusted with him.

"Of course, I know," he blabbed around some more. "It was at Billy Simonsen's house—don't you remember? That was the time you and Billy tipped the Victrola over. It sure was a swell party."

Breakfast over, Scoop and Red rowed our animals to the island, setting them loose to hunt for their own food, after which we all turned a hand to getting out the timbers for our proposed raft, it having been decided that we should go ahead with that job, as planned,, putting off our treasure hunt until later on.

Taking turns with the wrecking bar, we tore off a big patch of siding on the south part of the old building, thus showing up the timbers that formed its skeleton, or framework. It was these heavy timbers, all hand-hewn, that we needed for our raft. But it was no small job, I want to tell you, getting them out.

Having been given a written permit to tear down the old tavern, we kept this paper handy, as we went ahead with our work, figuring that Mr. Cadman would show up sooner or later to order us out. But to our surprise he never came near us. Later in the morning we learned from a farmer, who stopped to talk with us, that the former owner of the property was sick in bed.

"Calc'late you fellers must be lookin' fur somethin'," the visitor took in our work with inquisitive eyes.

"We're going to build a raft," Scoop informed.

"A raft, hey? What be you goin' to do with a raft?—ride on it?"

"Probably," said the leader, hiding a grin.

A shrewder look came into the man's eyes.

"Sure it hain't the King's Silver that you're huntin' fur?"

"Well," laughed Scoop, wiping his sweaty face, "if the silver does drop out of a hole in the wall we probably won't refuse to pick it up promptly."

"You might jest as well look fur a needle in a haystack," the farmer spit. "If that silver ever *was* hid, as they say, it'll stay hid till doomsday. Fur there's bin too many failures in searchin' fur it to make me think that it'll ever be found. . . . Ashton boys?" he spit again.

"No," said Scoop, spitting in pattern, "we're from Tutter."

"I've got a cousin livin' in Tutter. Used to tend bar, before the war. But now they tell me he's j'ined the Salvation Army."

"I think I know him," grinned Scoop. "He plays the drum."

"*Him* play a drum?" the farmer showed amazement. "I swan! Is he gittin' musical, too? . . . Campin' here?"

"We're friends of the man who bought the island," I spoke up.

"Oh! . . . The millionaire, hey? Hear he's goin' to fix the island up swell. Cadman got a big price fur it. Twenty thousand dollars! I wouldn't 'a' believed that he could 'a' sold it fur two thousand, let alone *twenty* thousand. But he always was lucky. Got this place fur nothin'. Give to him right out. They say he's worth a hundred thousand. But if I had to go 'round with a scart look on me like him—as though he expected any minute to have somethin' *grab* him by the windpipe an' start squeezin'—I'd ruther be poor.''

"But why should he be afraid of his windpipe?" I inquired, to draw the man out, thinking of what Mrs. Cassidy had told me.

"You tell *me,* sonny, an' I'll tell you. What *he* knows he keeps to hisself. Ever since he got this place there's bin talk of crooked work. I don't mean that he actually killed the old lady—she died naturally enough, as the doctors proved. It wasn't p'ison. But they was somethin' in connection with her death that never come out—an' Cadman *he* knows what that somethin' is. It's his secret. Anyway, that's my idear. . . . Don't s'pose any of you boys ever seed the old lady durin' her lifetime.''

"No," I told him.

"Wa-al, you missed somethin'. A queerer woman never lived. She had Cadman scart to death. Had queer powers over him. An' when she died *he* actually believed that she would come back. Now, hain't it ridiculous what tomfoolery some people will believe? I s'pose since the beginnin' of time people has talked, scart-like, about speerits an' ghosts.

But in all these thousands of years has anybody really *seed* a speerit or a ghost? Not
by a jugful. They hain't no sech thing. An'
that's why it's so ridiculous that ol' Miz Morrison should 'a' let herself believe that *she,*
in contradiction to the hul history of the world,
could come back, as she put it, from the grave.
No, sir, when people are put away in the
ground they stay put. The one thing they
don't do is to come back an' start spookifyin'.
It *was* queer, of course, that the ol' lady actually died when she said she would. An' because of that some superstitious people were
led to believe that other queer things would
happen. But nigh onto six years have passed
now since we put the ol' lady away, five feet
down, head to the east an' feet to the west,
an' no one has seed her speerit yet. Of course,
they's all kinds of queer stories told around
about Cadman. Him havin' the same belief—
voodooism, they call it—an' livin' in the same
house with her when she died, they say *he*
sees things, which may explain that scart look
of his'n. But, as I say, he never talks. It's
got so no housekeeper will stay there. So he
has to do his own housework—only my wife
is stayin' there now, as an accommodation,
him bein' down on his back an' unable to do
anything much fur himself. Mebbe we'll git

somethin' fur it an' mebbe we won't. But, as fur as *pay* is concerned, my wife, who is nervous, anyway, says she wouldn't stay there, an' make a regular job of it, fur all the money in the world. That's the way it is. People don't feel safe there. Even the new hired man goes around with a scart look, my wife says. . . . Wa-al, I hope you find it, boys," the farmer started off, with final reference to the lost silver. "But look out for ol' Cadman if you *do* find it."

Working with the wrecking bar and axe, together with two saws, which cut wood, we discovered, faster than old nails, we got out eight timbers that morning. Then, following dinner and a brief rest-up, during which we lay in the shade and suggested ways of spending Al's coming fortune, we set to work, with renewed strength, getting out another batch of timbers. Eighteen in all, we sawed them into equal lengths, in workmanlike manner, after which we "snaked" them to the canal bank, old Chris, of course, doing the pulling.

Then, selecting a level spot on the sandy beach, where we had enjoyed our morning swim, we placed the timbers, on rollers, side by side, one snug against the other, spiking them together with a plank at each end. This gave us the "body" of our raft. But for better footing, and to further improve the appearance of the job, we picked out the best of the old siding for a "deck," which, laid crosswise, was nailed fast to the timbers.

And were we proud of the finished job! Oh, baby! A peachier raft couldn't be imagined.

Having had the foresight to build it on rollers, as I say, we easily launched it. And then, of course, we wanted to try it out right away, and did. But the afternoon was too far gone to permit of any extended trip. Besides, we were all in. So it was decided that we should knock off and get supper, delaying our trip to the wreck, beyond the island, until the following morning. But to have everything in readiness for an early start, we cut four long willow "pushing" poles, further loading the raft, now safely anchored for the night, with our repair material.

The day, starting so splendidly, as described, ended in a drizzle, which, as I say, is the part of camping that I don't like. But a fellow has to make the best of such things. Besides, we were nice and dry in the old tavern. So there was nothing to kick about. Having plenty of wood, we liberally fed the flames, as the dripping darkness crowded in. Then we sat around the fire singing songs and telling stories.

A rig drove by shortly after nine o'clock. But the heavy darkness kept us from seeing anything in the road except the sickly yellow light of a moving lantern. Probably it was the farmer, we said, whose wife was staying with the sick man, or possibly a doctor. Then ten or fifteen minutes later we heard an automobile.

"Hot-dog!" yipped Red, when two men, in raincoats, stomped into the tavern. "Here's your pa, Jerry. I bet he's brought us some ice cream—hey, Mr. Todd?"

That's old hungry-face, for you. All he thinks about is his stomach.

"Well, how's tricks?" grinned Dad, mussing up my hair.

"Fine and dandy," I told him, wondering curiously, and with some anxiety, what had brought him here.

"Got your raft built?"

"We finished it just before supper."

"And what big job comes next?" he continued his friendly grin.

"We're going to raise the scow to-morrow . . . if you haven't come to take me home."

"We're on our way to the farmhouse to see Mr. Cadman," the unexpected visit was then explained to me. "Mother would have come along if it hadn't been raining. She put some stuff in the car for you. And Red's mother said to tell him——"

"To wash my ears, I suppose," the freckled listener piped up.

"No," grinned Dad. "She said to tell you your canary laid another egg this afternoon."

Red looked disgusted.

"As though *I* cared anything about an old canary egg—a hard-boiled guy like *me*. Geeminy crickets! Look me over, Mr. Todd—I'm Daniel Boone number two. . . . What'd Jerry's ma send?—cake?"

"It's a big package," laughed Dad.

"Come on," yipped Red, grabbing Al by the arm. "Let's go get it."

"Who's the strange boy?" Dad inquired, when the pair were out of hearing.

Al had told us his story in confidence.

"Oh," I said, kind of offhand-like, "he's a kid from Indiana."

"Rather good-looking."

"Yes," I nodded, "and he's just as good as he looks."

And now I learned something about the island that surprised me. Instead of actually owning it, as I had been led to believe, Mr. Cliffe only had an option on it. But this required no change in our plans, he said. For he and Dad were now on their way to the farm-house with a certified check for $19,500, the balance due, to close the deal.

"Cadman, queerly, tried to back out of the deal," Dad spoke up. "And as the option expires at midnight, Mr. Cliffe, unable to get a ten-day extension, had to make a special trip from St. Louis."

"Why didn't Randall come with him?" I inquired, naming Mr. Cliffe's son, who, as you will recall, played such an important part in the "Whispering Cave" book.

"I think Randall's in Chicago," said Dad.

Here Red and Al tumbled into the tavern with loaded arms.

"Six pies," old hungry-face sang out. "And three cakes. Um-yum! I hope the frosting's as thick as it looks. Just think, Jerry," he beamed, "this couldn't have happened if you were an orphan."

That kid! If he isn't the limit.

Inquiring about Mrs. Dexter, I learned from Dad that no attempt had been made to molest her valuable dish collection, which rather up-set my theory of the "hidden eyes."

Probably, after all, she was right, was my conclusion, as I got ready, with the others, to turn in for the night, Dad and Mr. Cliffe having gone on to the farmhouse.

CHAPTER VII

THE TRUNK IN THE ATTIC

WE found a big inner tube stretched across our front door the following morning, and pinned to the tube was a note in Dad's familiar handwriting.

"Who said horseshoes are lucky?" the note read. "Mr. Cliffe and I picked up one with thirteen nails in it. And as we have no use for an inner tube with thirteen holes in it (count 'em!), we're leaving it with you fellows as a souvenir.

"Having, with stupendous foresight, left our 'spare' at home on the Victrola (or some place), we had the sweet job on our hands of changing tubes in the rain. I'm writing this in your boudoir, as you lie stretched out here and there, at the mystic hour of midnight. Br-r-r-r! I think I hear a ghost in your cellaret—or is it Red begging in his sleep for something to eat? Anyway, for safety's sake, you'd better investigate. I wanted to wake you up, to introduce you to the tire pump, but Mr. Cliffe's kind heart saved you to your peaceful slumbers. He said to tell you that the deal went through O.K. That puts a grin on your faces, huh? Well, gang, have a good time.

"And don't be surprised if Mr. Cliffe shows up the latter part of the week with a party of men. Having heard so much about your wonderful cave, he's curious to see it. If he does get his district managers together, in an old-fashioned camping party (snakes under the bed, caterpillars in the hunter's stew, and everything as per usual), bu-lieve me, I'll be there with my hair in a braid, even if I have to close down the brickyard. For I like that kind of fun as well as you boys."

Later we saw the tracks in the mud where Dad and his friend had jacked up the car. And the wonder was to us, as we considered the extent of their work, that we had slept through it all. But boys are that way, I guess. Once asleep, especially after a toilsome day, they're not easily awakened. Still, I kind of wished that Dad had gotten me up. For I could have helped him.

There was a race now, on the heels of breakfast, to get started for the island, off the south shore of which a big job awaited us. And realizing that we might be kept busy at the wreck the better part of the day, we hurriedly got together a bag of sandwiches, putting in some cookies and one of Mother's choice pies.

But it turned out that these preparations were unnecessary. For overnight the Stricker gang, from home, knowing of our "Robinson Crusoe" plans, had taken possession of the island. And already, early as it was, we found them working on our scow, the gunwales and end decks of which were out of water, it being their intention to repair the scow and appropriate it for their own use.

They had two rowboats, which explained how they had made the trip to the island, and one of the gang (I counted six of them) was standing waist deep in the water. The others apparently were depending on him to nail a board over the rent in the scow's plank bottom. Then, using a pitcher pump that they had brought along, they hoped to pump the hull dry, thus lifting the scow from its muddy bed, after which the bottom could be further repaired.

As I have written down in preceding books, we don't like the Stricker gang. For they aren't on the square, least of all Bid Stricker, the leader, who lives in a tough part of Tutter called Zulutown. Instead of providing fun of their own, they'd rather steal some one else's fun. I guess, though, they aren't smart enough to think up anything original.

Evidently on the lookout for us, the enemy

hooted when we came into sight with our raft. But we, in turn, could only stare at them, so great was our surprise at finding them there. We never had dreamed of such a thing.

"What is it?" jeered Bid, referring to our raft, which, I'll admit, was rather clumsy and tiresome to handle. "The wreck of the *Hesperus?*"

"Maybe it's the *Flying Dutchman*," put in Jimmy Stricker, who also lives in Zulutown.

"Or Noah's ark," was the brilliant contribution of Hib Milden, still another Zuluite.

Bid balanced himself on the scow's gunwale.

"I can't see Noah," said he, pretending that he had a telescope. "But I guess it's the ark, all right. For I can see two jackasses and three monkeys."

"That red-headed one that you see isn't a monkey," Hib corrected. "It's a gorilla."

"You'll both see yourselves in pine boxes with clever glass tops," bellowed Peg, recovering from his surprise, "if you don't put a clothespin on your gab and get out of here. Who do you think you are, anyway?"

Bid performed on the gunwale.

"Look us over, liver-and-onions," he puffed out his chest. "We're the Surprise Salvage Company. *You* get the surprise, and *we* get the salvage. See?"

"Why don't you stay at home for once," said Scoop, disgusted, "and tend to your own business?"

"Why should we?" said Bid. "You guys don't own the canal."

"Maybe not. But we own that scow."

"Oh, no you don't. It used to be yours— and mighty smart you thought yourselves, too, when you were riding around in it. But it's ours now."

"You tell that to my father," I yipped, "and see what *he* says."

A part of his brickyard equipment, and used years ago for hauling clay, but of use no longer, big clay trucks having taken its place, Dad had cheerfully turned the old scow over to us. I told about that in the "Oak Island Treasure" book, in which story, you will recall, we fitted up our show boat, the *Sally Ann,* with a power plant, consisting of an old automobile engine and a home-made wooden propeller. It wasn't much to look at. But it worked. And the noise made by the combined engine and propeller was *wonderful.*

"According to marine law," said Bid, talking big, "the scow is ours, no matter who its former owners were. And we intend to keep it, too. So just put that in your pipe and smoke it."

"A lot *you* know about marine law," sneered Scoop.

"The law is," Bid further spread his intelligence around, "that when a vessel is abandoned it becomes the property of anybody who wants to claim it."

"Yah, a *vessel*."

"Well, that's what this is. And having salvaged it, after you abandoned it, we claim ownership."

"Now, look here, Bid," said Peg, "you should have sense enough to know that you can't get away with that."

"*Him* have sense?" Red put in. "Don't make me laugh."

"Go ahead and laugh," bellowed Bid. "You can't make yourself look any homelier than the rest of your ancestors in the zoo."

"*Oh!* . . ." screamed Red, dancing and shaking his fists. "What I'll do to you when I get my mitts on you."

"Yah, sweetie," simpered Bid, posing on the gunwale.

"Gee," said Red, "wouldn't I love to give him a shove!"

"The scow is ours," Peg went on. "And if we can't get it any other way we'll fight for it."

Bid screwed up his face contemptuous-like.

"Oh, you don't say so. I suppose you think we're scared of you."

"You ought to know us by this time."

"What do you mean by that?"

"We've cleaned up on you before. And we can do it again."

"Your luck won't last forever. Besides, we've got you outnumbered."

"We own that scow," Peg maintained. "And we're going to get it."

"Come and take it," Bid dared.

"We can do it."

"Try it, and see what you get."

"Yes," put in Jimmy eagerly, "go ahead and try it."

Al got Peg's ear.

"Look out for 'em. They're armed."

"You bet your sweet life we're armed," cried Bid, whose sharp ears had picked up the words.

"Let's pepper 'em," cried Jimmy.

"All right," consented Bid. "Load up, gang. Are you ready? One, two, three, *fire*."

Every last one of them had a slingshot. And we hadn't anything with which to defend ourselves, not even a handful of pebbles.

"Ouch!" squealed Red, as a plump acorn socked him in the breadbasket.

"Aim low," shouted Bid, directing the bombardment, "and pull hard. Are you ready? One, two, three, *fire.*"

It was a lucky thing for us that they were shooting acorns instead of pebbles. For, be it said to their credit, their aim was almost perfect. Of course, we could have saved ourselves to some extent by dropping flat on the raft. But it was important, we figured, to get out of range. And to do that we had to stand up and work, the sweat streaming down our faces.

"The next time," Bid yelled after us, "you'll get a dose of the real stuff. And if pebbles won't stop you, we'll use bricks."

"I feel sorry for you, Bid," Peg grimly wiped his face. "What you're going to get! Oh, baby! It's worth waiting for."

"Bla, bla, bla."

We took it easier when we were out of their sight behind the island.

"Of all the rotten luck," said Scoop, looking sick and disgusted.

"Who are they?" Al inquired curiously. "Enemies of yours?"

"You should know that without asking," growled Scoop. And then, realizing that this was no way to answer a friend, he told in detail who the Strickers were, and why they had cut in on us.

Landing on Tavern Beach, as we now called that section of the shore, we made our raft safe, with a rope, after which we gathered up our stuff and trailed dejectedly through the forest.

"I'd like to sock Hib Milden with a rock," growled Red, as we crossed the clearing, where old Chris was contentedly filling himself up on weeds. "Did you hear what he called me?"

Peg grinned.

"Don't let that bother you, kid. For you can't help it if you look that way."

"Say! . . ." Red began to dance. "For two cents I'd sock *you.*"

"You'd better save your strength," grunted Scoop. "For I have a hunch that you're going to need it before we get the upper hands of that gang. Blame the old luck, anyway."

Peg got his eyes on the inner tube.

"Oh, baby!" he cried, as an idea came to him. "If they want slingshot stuff, let's give it to them in big gobs."

"What do you mean?" Scoop asked quickly.

"Let's make a slingshot that *is* a slingshot," grinned Peg, running the tube through his fingers.

"With *that?*"

"Sure thing."

"But can we do it? Will it work?"

"Why shouldn't it work? Here's the rubber for the bands. And we have plenty of big crotches handy."

Agreeing that it was a corking good scheme, and undoubtedly would gain for us the victory that we longed for, we decided to make the big slingshot right away, giving it the very appropriate name of "Big Bertha," which, as you may know, is the name sometimes given to a huge cannon. As for ammunition, what would better suit our needs, Scoop said, than nice soft clay balls.

So we split up, the leader heading into the forest with the axe to get the needed crotch, which was to be mounted on the raft in regular gunboat style, while Red and Al hurried back to the canal to roll clay balls. Needing a leather "pouch" for the slingshot, and learning from Al that there was an accumulation of junk in the attic, I ran upstairs, at Peg's suggestion, to see what I could find, discovering that while we were away a section of the roof had caved in.

But I didn't let that stop me. And a moment later, having shinned up Al's rope ladder, I found myself in the attic, formerly a dark hole, but now as light as day, thanks to the hole in the roof.

A place like that always fires a boy's curiosity, suggesting, as it does, things of possible value, left behind and forgotten. So, when I spied an old trunk, close under the eaves, in what had been the darkest corner of the attic, my first glad thought was that I had crossed the trail of the lost silver.

But to my disappointment the trunk, the rotten lid of which fell to pieces in my hands, contained mostly old clothing, with no trace of the coveted silver.

Yet what *peculiar* clothing. It took me several minutes to comprehend that I was looking at the garments of the pirate whose earrings Al had dug out of the cellar floor.

Well, though of little value, this was an interesting find. And yelling to Peg to come and help me, we lowered the trunk through the trapdoor to the upper hall floor.

"I know what we'll do," cried Peg, spreading the old garments around. "We'll dress up like pirates. More than that," his enthusiasm carried him along, "we'll *be* pirates. Then, oh, boy, how we'll fight! We'll show those birds a thing or two. *Look!* Here's an old cutlass. I bet it's whacked off more heads than Bid Stricker has fingers and toes. Um. . . . I can almost smell the blood on the blade. Of course, dull as it is, it wouldn't cut putty now. But that's all right. Bid and his gang never will know from the looks of it that it isn't sharp. And how they'll beg for their lives when we get the upper hand of them. Will they walk the plank? Nothing else but. Boy, this is going to be fun. Pirates! I'm really glad, Jerry, that they butted in on us. But what a sad, sad 'butt' it was for them, as they'll soon find out.''

At the very bottom of the trunk, sort of hid away, I found a small leather-backed book, the pages of which were yellow with age. And so dim was the handwriting in places that I could barely make out the words, all of which were written in English.

Then, as the truth of my discovery dawned on me, I caught my breath.

"*Peg!*" I cried. "It's the lost diary."

"And what does that mean?" the other inquired, slow to realize our amazing good fortune.

"If Al's story is true," I cried, with increasing excitement, "it means that we're on the trail of the long-lost King's Silver."

Then we dashed down the stairs, to the lower floor, having heard something below us that sounded like stealthy footfalls.

But the rooms were empty.

CHAPTER VIII

WHAT WE FOUND IN THE SPRING

We knew, all right, that we had made a big find. There was no doubt about that. For there was stuff written down in the back of the diary, mostly about the drugged hunchback, that matched Al's story perfectly.

Yet, when Peg and I learned the truth about the silver's hiding place we stared at each other in amazement.

No wonder the treasure had remained undiscovered all these years! For a stranger or more unusual hiding place couldn't be imagined.

Calling the others in from their work we showed them the diary, telling them how we had found it hidden away in the bottom of the pirate's trunk.

Al at first was so stupefied by his unexpected good fortune that he could hardly talk. But when he got his voice a happier kid I never hope to see.

"Oh, gee!" he cried. "Just think of it— I'm going to be rich. *Me,* mind you—the poorest kid in Indiana. Now I can have a bicycle and a rifle. And I can go to high school and college." Singling me out with his happy eyes he added feelingly: "It sure was a happy moment for me, Jerry, when you spotted that old trunk."

"You must have been blind," Red spoke up in his blunt way, "not to have seen the trunk, yourself. Didn't you ever search the attic?"

"Sure thing. But all I had was a candle."

"And you never noticed the trunk?"

"No."

"Which isn't to be wondered at," I put in. "For the trunk was shoved back under the eaves. Besides, there was no light up there until the roof caved in."

Scoop gave a puzzled laugh.

"Well, it certainly was a lucky thing for you," he told Al, "that the roof didn't collapse when some other searching party was on the job. That's all I've got to say."

Possibly, like the leader, you're now thinking to yourself, sort of clever-like, that it was mighty queer, to say the least, that the pirate's trunk had remained undiscovered all these years. Considering the many times that the old tavern has been searched from top to bottom, by members of the family and other treasure hunters, it's your notion that some one, possibly more observing or more thorough than the others, should have made the important discovery ahead of me. More than that, the diary should have been found before the trunk was put away in the attic, there to be abandoned, as you might say, and in time completely forgotten.

Well, as a matter of fact, as you will learn through later developments, the trunk held a bigger secret than any of us suspected. A mystery trunk! That's what it was. We found that out. Remember, too, about the footfalls that Peg and I heard.

Queer things were going on around us.

According to the old diary, which was then read to us in part by the leader, the silver had been put away in the near-by marsh, on a "rocky knoll," which, of course, was the place that we now called Oak Island. There was mention of a moonlit winding cow-path—a path leading through the marsh—along which the silver had been carried by its frantic owner. Then, according to the diary—and this was the most surprising part of all—the treasure had been dropped into the big spring, piece by piece, where it quickly sank from sight in the bubbling sand.

"For the love of mud!" squeaked Red, when the secret was out. "The old lady must have been cuckoo. For whoever heard of anybody in their right senses hiding stuff in a *spring?* Why," he wound up, thinking of the quicksand in the bottom of the spring, "the silver may be halfway to China by this time."

But it was Scoop's opinion that the quicksand wasn't more than two or three feet deep. No doubt, like most springs, this one had a hard bottom, where the water oozed through cracks in the rocks. So, if we could rig up some kind of a grab-pole, about five feet long, how easy for us to "pick up" the silver piece by piece. It would take considerable feeling around, and hence considerable time. But that was nothing.

So we put aside the big slingshot for the time being, figuring that it was more important to recover the sunken treasure. Scoop was the boss. A lot of his mechanical ideas were punk. But we finally got a pole rigged up that worked.

Yet, this would be useless to us if the quicksand was more than three feet deep. And realizing that a longer pole was impracticable, we wondered, in the event of failure, if it would be possible to pump the spring dry, quicksand and all.

Red said we were crazy. It would be just as easy, he blatted, to dig a post hole in the middle of the Illinois River. To shut him up,

Peg took after him with the grab-pole, which, I might explain, was a sort of long-handled "fist" worked by a lever like a tree pruner.

"Ouch!" danced freckle face, when the "fist" nipped him in the seat of the pants. "Loosen up, you big cow. I'm not made of cast iron."

"If it works that good in the quicksand," laughed Scoop, rescuing his pet invention, "we ought to come home at daybreak with our coffers full of silver."

"*Coffers!*" bellowed Red, feeling of himself. Then he glared at Peg. "They'll need a *coffin* for you, big boy."

But old hefty just laughed in his good-natured way. And soon he and the freckled one were fooling around as friendly as ever. So, as you can see, however much we may squabble back and forth, particularly Red and Peg, it would be a mistake to take us seriously. It's all in fun. When danger threatens we stick together like glue, any one of us ready to go through fire and water to help the others.

Beyond the island the Strickers were hard at work. We could hear them hammering and pumping. Then late in the afternoon we caught the familiar sound of our old motor.

Presently the scow came slowly and gracefully into sight around the island's west end, the motor wheezing and the propeller chattering in its worn wooden bearings.

And did Bid ever act big!

"Look at 'em," he jeered, catching sight of us on Tavern Beach. "They're green with envy."

"Yah," said Jimmy, "they're *green*, all right."

They didn't know about the treasure in the spring. And that to us was a thousand times more important than an old scow. So the situation wasn't half as galling to us as they suspected.

Anyway, we had a few tricks up our sleeves, as they were going to discover to their sorrow before very many hours had passed.

"What is it?" Red jeered in turn, not to be outdone by the others. "A cargo of donkeys?"

Bid put a hand to his right ear.

"Louder," he shouted. "I can't hear you."

"Get a shovel and clean out your ears."

"Huh?"

"Or if you can't find a shovel use a manure fork."

"Huh?"

"You'll look like a 'huh,' all right, when we get through with you."

"What?"

"Aw, shut up," Red lost patience.

"Pup?" Bid pretended to misunderstand. "What pup? What do you mean?"

"SHUT UP."

"Huh?"

Then, to further show off, the triumphant leader balanced himself on the narrow gunwale like a tight-rope walker. He sure was silly. And did we ever laugh when the scow struck a sunken log, shooting the performer into the shallow water, where, for a moment or two, he stuck upside-down in the mud.

But he soon righted himself.

"Hey," he yelled to his gang. "Come back and pick me up."

"Louder," mimicked Red. "We can't quite hear you."

"Aw, shut up. I wasn't talking to you."

"Pup?" chirped Red, in further mimicry. "What pup? What are you talking about?"

"SHUT UP."

"Huh?"

Bid then yelled to Hib Milden to stop the motor.

"I can't stop it," the engineer yelled back

"Turn the switch."

"I did turn it."

"And won't it stop?"

"No."

"Oh, gee!" gurgled Red. "They don't know

that there's two switches. I rigged it up.''

Hib could have stopped the motor by disconnecting the spark-plug wires. But he wasn't smart enough to think of that. So for more than ten minutes the scow went around and around in a wide circle. Bid tried to climb aboard. But he had no luck until the motor swallowed an overdose of gasoline, or something, and gagged itself to death.

Which reminded me of times when it had done the same thing with us. And what a job we had had getting it started! It was a nice motor, all right. I don't want to knock it. But at the same time I can't deny that it had some mean ways. Still, with all of its faults, we were hopeful that the enemy wouldn't smash it up on us.

Bid sure was a sight when he crawled aboard. All I could think of was a hog fresh from a mud hole.

''Why didn't you stop when I told you?'' he flew at Hib.

''Couldn't.''

''I ought to sock you.''

''Hey, Bid,'' chirped Peg. ''Please do it over again, won't you? We want to take your picture.''

''Yah,'' put in Red, ''we want to publish it in the *Hog Wallow Review*.''

"Shut up, I tell you."

"We'll pay you, Bid."

"SHUT UP."

Hib tried to start the motor. But it wouldn't percolate. And now was the time when we could have made good use of our big slingshot. However, there was no hurry about that. Other chances would come up later on.

Taking turns, Bid and his gang cranked for more than an hour. But with no success. So finally they gave up in disgust.

"Haw, haw, haw!" we hooted in chorus, as they got out their poles and began pushing.

While Scoop and I were getting supper the others gathered more raspberries, which gave our evening meal a dandy finishing touch. Then we fooled around playing "duck on the rock" and other games until the sun went down. We could see a fire through the trees on the island. But the enemy was too tired to make much noise. And when the fire finally died down at nine-thirty, and silence settled over the island, we had every reason to believe that its occupants had turned in for the night.

Now was our chance. But to make sure that the enemy wasn't hiding along the shore, in anticipation of a secret attack, we waited another hour, in perfect silence. Then, having agreed upon a plan, Scoop and I set out in the

water-logged skiff, the others having been instructed to wait on Tavern Beach for our later
signal.

By using the lighter craft the leader and I
could make a quicker get-away, in case of danger. And if we found no trace of the silver
the others would thus be saved a toilsome trip
across the wide waters. However, if we did
find the treasure, as was our big hope, and
everything was safe on the island, it was
agreed that we were to signal across the water
with our flashlight, after which the others
were to man the raft and join us with as little
delay as possible.

It was a thrilling adventure. And I had a
queer tremor inside of me as we set forth.
Years ago the King's Silver had been put
away in the moonlight. And now we were going to recover it in the moonlight.

At least we were going to try.

The deep silence continued on the island.
But, as Scoop said, however much this seemed
to favor our plans, it would be wisest to guard
against possible prying eyes. So, instead of
following a direct course across the moonlit
lake we paddled up the shore, in the shadow
of the trees and bushes, finally landing on the
island's extreme east end. Securing our skiff
we then started off with the grab-pole in the

direction of the spring, keeping to the shore as much as possible, though in places where the rocks shut us off we had to do considerable climbing. Somewhere near here was the sub-terranean entrance of the big cave that we had discovered. And it had been our plan, in re-turning to the island, to enlarge this opening, so that we could use Owl Pool, within, as a sort of underground harbor. I wondered curi-ously, as I climbed over the rocks, if the now submerged entrance had been visible before the canal was built.

To make sure of our safety Scoop crept through the bushes to the south shore, where the enemy's tents were pitched, having in-structed me to wait at the spring.

"Well?" I breathed, when he came back from the silent camp.

"Everybody's asleep except Hib Milden."

"Standing guard?"

"Trying to. But he's more'n half asleep."

"Hot dog! I have a good notion to signal to our chums right away."

"No, let's wait, as agreed, and see if there's anything here."

"What do *you* think?" I asked him curi-ously, as he took the grab-pole and went over to the spring.

"I have big hopes, Jerry."

"Anyway," I said, as my heart continued to jump around, "it's blamed exciting."

Six feet across at the widest point, and shaped like an egg, the big spring, with its rocky walls and bubbling quicksand, lay mirror-like in the moonlight. . . . I never realized before that there was something spooky about a moonlit spring. There seemed to be tremendous power here—power that gave out not the slightest sound. My heart thumped harder than ever.

Down, down went the pole.

"Strike bottom?" I breathed.

"Sure thing."

"Hard?"

"Solid rock."

"Sandstone, I bet."

"Probably."

"Feel anything?"

"No."

"Want me to try?"

"Just a minute. I felt something that time."

"Work your lever."

"Rats!"

"What's the matter?"

"Missed."

The pole was then handed to me.

"There's something down there, all right," I

prodded. "Boy, if only I could get at it with my hands!"

"Try over here," said Scoop, moving to the other side of the spring.

"Rocks," I told him, after more prodding.

"Sugar bowls and cups," said he, "would seem like rocks. . . . Can't you grab it?"

"Hot-dog!" I cried. "I've got it."

Then up came the pole, inch by inch.

"A *plate*," cried Scoop, as the treasure fell at our feet. "A silver plate. Oh, gee! Won't Al be tickled! Just think of it, Jerry—the long-lost King's Silver has been found at last."

CHAPTER IX

The sensible part of my head had been telling me on our way here to prepare myself for disappointment. For, as Red had said, no one but a crazy woman would hide her valuable silver in a spring. Crazy people aren't dependable. So the diary, so exciting to us at the start, could very well turn out to be a bunch of junk.

Still, as the preceding chapter shows, I hadn't let these thoughts cramp my enthusiasm. Not for one moment. In fact, for the most part, I was hardly conscious that I had such thoughts.

So, if such a thing were possible, I was even more excited than Scoop over our recovery of the silver plate. Certainly, I was happier. For success had come where I had partly looked for failure. Oh, gee! How lucky we were! Al was a good kid. I wanted to see him succeed. And now he had the world by the tail. A hundred thousand dollars' worth of silver! *Some* treasure. Why, there wasn't a richer boy in the whole state of Illinois. That is, he *would* be a rich boy when the rest of the treasure had been lifted and turned into money.

The plate, of course, didn't look like silver. To tell the truth, it was as black as our old frying pan. But when we scraped the recovered dish with a pocketknife—oh, baby! The shine was there. And the heft, too. So don't get the mistaken idea that we had fished up a pie tin that some camper had dropped into the spring. Not on your life. A solid silver dish, and nothing else but. Besides, it was covered with fancy designs. In one place we could make out the shape of a crown. A *crown*, mind you. Get that. So we knew, beyond all doubt, that it was indeed a part of the long-lost treasure.

Well, having found one dish there was no reason why we couldn't find more. It was simply a matter of patient search. So we got busy with the grab-pole, though first we signaled across the water to our waiting chums, contented in the thought of how happy Al would be to thus learn of our success.

And now comes the part of my story that I hate to write down, telling as it does how completely our luck had deserted us and, further, how brimful, so to speak, was our cup of gall. For what do you know if Bid Stricker and his tricky gang weren't lying in the weeds watching us. Their "sentinel" was just a blind. Patroling the island's north shore, in anticipation of a midnight attack, they had spotted us

in the skiff and later had watched us land.
Puzzled to understand where our chums were,
and suspicious of a trick, they had held back.
And how richly this had profited them you can
figure out for yourself. Not only had they
seen us lift the silver plate from its watery
hiding place, but having overheard our talk they
now knew that more treasure of a like nature
was concealed in the spring. Moreover, they
had seen us signal to our chums.

So, ready for us now, they suddenly rushed
upon us from behind. Gee! Nervous anyway,
as I have mentioned, I almost jumped out of
my skin. Then, seeing who it was, and realizing what we were up against, I tried to fight
my way out. But it was no use. We were
hopelessly outnumbered. And worst of all they
shoved me into the spring.

Going under, head and all, I had the horrible
panicky feeling that the quicksand was sucking
me down. It seemed so. But that was all imagination. When I got turned around, with
my head on top where it belonged, I found that
the quicksand was only about two feet deep.
And below the sand there was firm hard footing. So, with my head and shoulders out of
water, I was in no danger of drowning. But
was I ever *co-o-old!* Gee-miny crickets gosh!
I thought I'd freeze to death. Yet Bid, the big

bully, thought it was funny. He even asked me to pose like a fountain statue and squirt water through my mouth.

Scoop was lucky. All they did to him was to sock him on the bean and gag him to keep him from yelling a warning to our chums, who were crossing the wide waters on the raft.

Taking pity on me, Bid finally let me crawl out of the spring. Or, rather, he had Hib Milden's brother drag me out. For it's a fact I was too near the icicle stage to help myself. As for yelling to my chums, I couldn't even say "cat." My chattering teeth sounded like a riveting machine.

Bid, of course, was in his glory. Usually a sufferer at our hands, we being the smartest, he was getting the best of us in every way. First he had successfully snitched the scow on us. And now he had the two of us completely in his power, with the prospects of further easy captures. If he had owned 768 gilded horseshoes his luck couldn't have been more perfect. As for us, as I say, we had no luck at all.

"Well," he leered at me in his mean way, "how do you like it? Getting some of your own medicine, huh?"

And poor shivering wretch that I was, all I could say was, "Bu-u-u-u-u."

"Go ahead and sing, if you want to," he made fun of me. "We can stand it if you can."

"Bu-u-u-u-u," I further rattled my teeth.

"He thinks he's a human rattlebox," Jimmy Stricker piped up.

"Bu-u-u-u-u."

"I believe it's a habit," Bid kind of leaned toward me.

"Bu-u-u-u-u."

"Let's look at your palate, jello-face. Maybe it needs adjusting."

Then the leader's attention was drawn to Chet Milden, who had picked up the silver dish near the spring.

"No," Bid corrected the other, "it isn't lead. It's solid silver."

"*That?*" Chet looked at the dish scornfully.

"Sure thing."

"Who ever saw silver that color."

"You'd be black, too," said Bid, "if you'd been in the spring as long as that dish has."

"What do you mean?"

"I don't suppose you ever heard the story of the King's Silver."

"No."

"Well, I have. For my mother was raised around here."

"What of it?"

"This is a part of it."

"A part of what?"

"The King's Silver."

"Is it worth anything?" Chet began to show more respect for the plate.

"*Is* it? Say, kid, if we can find the whole set we'll be millionaires. . . . But there's other work to be done before we can start treasure hunting. Here, take these prisoners back to camp and tell Hib to keep a close eye on them. Then prepare yourselves for a real battle. For you know Peg Shaw. He'll fight like a demon. And that other new kid, too, I imagine."

"I can hear them coming. They've got the raft. *See?* There they are."

"Skip," Bid gave the sharp command. "And tell Hib to use plenty of ropes and gags. The more the better. Oh, baby! The King's Silver! I never dreamed of any such luck as this. It's worth a fortune, fellows."

"But who put it in the spring?—pirates?"

"Sh-h-h-h! I can't tell you now. Action, gang. *Action.* What'd I tell you. Step on it."

I was miserable in my wet clothes. So our jailer let me strip and wrap myself in a blanket. Hating to be gagged, I promised to keep my mouth shut. But Hib wouldn't trust me. Anyway, as he explained, he had to obey orders. And there we were, completely in the enemy's power, one of us stark naked, with goose pimples as big as pancakes, and both of us double trussed and gagged.

Having turned us over to Hib, the others, in keeping with Bid's orders, had chased back to the spring. And now they were lying in ambush. Oh, if only some kind Providence would warn our unsuspecting chums; if only *we* could warn them. Having gotten our favorable signal, they probably were poling for dear life, eager to get to the spring to view the recovered treasure. It wouldn't be many minutes before they landed. And then——

Suddenly the island's deep silence was broken by a chorus of shouting voices.

"It's a trap," bellowed Peg. "Scoop and Jerry aren't here."

"Go for 'em," thundered Bid. "Sock 'em on the head."

"Oh, you're going to sock us, huh? How do you like that, you big stiff? And here's one more for good measure."

Bid squealed like a cornered rat.

"Hel-lp! He's killing me."

Was our big chum cleaning up on the whole gang? It would seem so from the sounds that reached us. My heart bounded with joy. Good old Peg!

Then, as the fight continued, with Red getting in a characteristic squawk now and then, we heard more and more triumphant shouts from the enemy. Our chums were getting the worst of it. It was sickening to me, considering all that was at stake. Still, with so few on one side and so many on the other, it was to be expected.

Hib cut the strings that held our gags.

"Now," said he, "yell, if you want to."

But what good would that do us? Our chums were prisoners like ourselves. Instead of yelling, we groaned in despair.

"What were you fellows trying to do?" Hib then inquired curiously. "Capture the island?"

I stared at him. Then, remembering that he hadn't been out of camp, and hence knew nothing about the treasure in the spring, a daring scheme flashed into my mind.

If one of us could get away, to summon help, we could turn the tables on the Strickers within an hour. For the towns of Steam Corners and Ashton, on either side of us, were only a few miles away. And the county sheriff would help us. For the Strickers were trespassers.

"Hib," I panted excitedly.

"Well?"

"I've got to get away from here before Bid gets back."

He gave a scornful laugh.

"Is that a joke?"

"No," I got down to business, realizing that I hadn't a second to spare, "it's a bribe."

He searched my face.

"What do you mean?"

"Did I ever tell you a lie?"

"Not that I know of."

"And if I promised to pay you a hundred dollars, would you believe me?"

"A *hundred dollars?*" he repeated, further studying me in the moonlight.

"In cash," I nodded.

"Honest, cross your heart?"

"I hope to die."

"I'll catch Hail Columbia from Bid."

"A hundred dollars is a hundred dollars, you know, Hib."

"And you really mean it?" his eyes grew greedy.

"On my honor."

His suspicions were aroused.

"But why are you so anxious to get away?"

"I can't tell you that," I evaded.

"A hundred dollars," he considered.

"Quick, Hib," I cried, my heart thumping. "Here they come."

But he seemed unable to come to a decision.

"Gosh! If I only dared."

"You know me, Hib," I urged. "When I say a thing I mean it."

"Yes," came another voice, "we know *you,* all right." And who should step into sight, in the moonlight, but Bid, himself. "I suspected this," he turned angrily on the jailer. "You dirty traitor."

"I didn't do anything," Hib whined, with a pasty look in his face.

"No you didn't *do* anything. But you probably would have done something if I hadn't happened along just in time."

"Aw! . . ."

"Shut up. For two cents I'd kick you out of my gang. You haven't any brains, anyway."

"What can you expect," Scoop spoke up daringly, "when he chums around with you?"

"Say. . . . I'll knock your block off."

"My, aren't you brave!"

"You better shut up if you know what's good for you."

"News item for the sporting page: 'The undaunted Bid Stricker tied Scoop Ellery hand and foot and heroically knocked his block off.' "

"Shut up, I tell you."

"I'm sorry Jerry didn't get away."

"Yah, I bet you are. And I know *why* he wanted to get away. But schemes of that kind don't work when I'm around."

Here the other three prisoners were dragged into camp. Yet, battered and worn out as they were, their eyes lit up at sight of us. That is, Peg's eyes lit up. Red, poor kid, couldn't see out of his eyes.

"Now, let me tell you something," Bid roughly addressed us in a group, his gang forming a circle. "One more funny stunt like Jerry just tried to pull on Hib and the whole bunch of you will be strung up by the heels. Do you get me? Submit quietly and you're safe. Try to escape and you're doomed. Oh, you think I'm bluffing, huh?" his face hardened. "Well, there's thousands of dollars in this for us if we work it right. There's no law on buried treasure. It belongs to whoever finds it. So, if there's more silver in the spring, we're going to get it. And until we *do* get it, for the sake of convenience, you guys are going to wear ropes."

We slept that night under guard. And when breakfast was under way the following morning we were told that Bid was on his way to Tutter to sell the silver plate to Mrs. Dexter and dicker with her for the rest of the set.

CHAPTER X

ADDED MYSTERY

Scoop and I had told the others about our recovery of the silver dish at the spring and the enemy's later surprise attack in which we had been taken prisoners. Without a doubt, we agreed, the complete treasure was hidden in the spring. Just as the diary said. For we had felt the dishes while prodding around with our pole.

And the others, in turn, had told us about their merry trip across the moonlit lake. Al in particular, we learned, had bubbled with joy. The treasure was found! Riches were his! He couldn't get to the island fast enough.

Push hard, fellows. Push with all your might. That, we were told, is the way he had urged the others on. And they had been more than willing. In fact, it was their eagerness to see the recovered treasure which largely led to their undoing. For when they finally landed on the island's north shore, where the second attack took place, they were winded.

Still, they had given Bid and his gang a hard battle. Both sides bore evidence of that. I've already mentioned Red's black eyes. He contends to this day that somebody laid him out with a baseball bat and then jumped on him. More probably, though, he ran into a tree. However, to do a little crowing on our side, it wasn't a tree that gave Bid *his* black eyes. Ask Peg for details!

Though showing the marks of battle, as I say, Bid's warriors generously shared their breakfast with us, freeing our hands so that we could eat. Some of the stuff they brought us wasn't much, especially the coffee, which had dead ants in it. But we made no complaints.

And then, having eaten, they again tied our hands behind our backs, that being Bid's orders, Hib explained, as he and Chet, the appointed guards, pulled the knots tight.

It's misery for a fellow to be tied up that way. Yet Peg, I noticed, said never a word. *He* can stand anything. But it was hard on Red. The poor kid. Much as he sickens me at times with his silly gab and homely face I now had a lot of sympathy for him. For he *was* kind of small.

Bid's memory hadn't failed him. Once before, as recorded in the "Whispering Cave" book, luck having favored him, he had taken us prisoners. Having read that story you prob-

ably will recall the details of our thrilling escape, from under the very nose of the guard,
as you might say, and our later flight across
the moonlit island. This time, however, we
were given no chance to secretly untie each
other's ropes, as before, the enemy chief having further instructed his guards to keep us
well separated.

So, as you can see, things looked pretty dark
for us, or, more particularly, for Al. If Bid's
gang lifted the complete treasure ahead of us
they probably would be permitted to keep it,
notwithstanding the fact that we had found
the treasure first. For they say that possession is nine points of law. Our helplessness
was sickening. Scoop, though, wouldn't give
up. There was still a way out, he declared,
putting his wits to work.

Bid's cousin had been placed in charge of
the camp with instructions to drain the spring
that morning and pile the recovered treasure
in one of the tents, ready for the leader's return. But before going to work Jimmy
meandered over to the "prison" to pump us.

"How did you kids find out that the silver
was hidden in the spring?" he began curiously,
wanting, no doubt, to pick up as much information as possible to pass along to the leader
upon the latter's return.

Still game, as I say, and confident that something would turn up to give us a fighting chance, Scoop winked at Peg.

"Shall we tell him?"

"Why not?" consented old hefty, realizing, of course, that our leader had no intention of giving away any important secrets.

"I suppose," Scoop began, "that you know who hid the silver there in the first place, and also where it came from."

"Sure thing," nodded Jimmy, kind of important-like. "Bid told us about it. The silver came from England, where, years ago, it was given to an old lady by the king, himself. That is how it got its name. A hunchback tried to steal it. So the old lady, or some other old lady—I don't remember which—hid it, after which the hunchback murdered her with a butcher knife."

"I never heard that she was murdered," said Scoop. "But it must be so if you say so. Anyway," he began making up stuff, as a scheme took shape in his mind, "that would explain why the hunchback wanted to borrow our soap. His hands were red. See? Peg thought it was paint. But probably, as you say, it was human blood."

"It looked like paint," Peg trustingly helped the leader along. "Didn't it, Jerry?"

"Sure thing," I put in.

"Say," Jimmy stared, too dumb to tumble

to the fact that we were stuffing him. "What in Sam Hill are you guys talking about?"

"Soap," Scoop smiled sweetly. "The hunchback wanted to borrow our soap. See? I just told you. And when we complied he gave us a hoot-nannie."

"A *which?*" Jimmy further stared.

"A hoot-nannie. Haven't you got one?"

"Oh, you big nut!"

"If not," Scoop pretended that it was a matter of great importance, "you're going to be out of luck. For every treasure hunter, to be successful, must carry a hoot-nannie. Not only does it bring its owners good luck, but it's protection against ghosts. The hunchback said so."

"What hunchback are you talking about?"

"The one who murdered the old lady."

"He's been dead fifty years."

"Of course. He told us all about it while he was washing his bloody hands. And then Jerry swallowed a horsefly. He was snoring. See? Along came the hunchback. Would we *please* lend him some soap? Sure thing. Nothing like being neighborly, you know. Then he gave us a hoot-nannie, explaining that it would bring us good luck. After which Jerry woke up . . . and it was all a dream."

Jimmy fancied that he saw daylight.

"And did Jerry dream that the silver was hidden in the spring?" he inquired eagerly.

"Say, Jimmy," Scoop dodged the question, "are you any good at guessing riddles?"

"*Now* what?"

"Here's a good one: Upon a hill there is a mill—that's the first syllable; in front of the mill there is a walk—the second syllable; and under the walk there is a key—the third syllable, the whole of which is the name of the largest city in Wisconsin. Now, see if you can guess it."

"Cambridge," said Jimmy, figuring, I guess, that the quickest way to end the crazy nonsense and get the actual facts of the case was by joining in.

"Correct," Scoop beamed. "Kid, you're smarter than I thought."

"Oh, I'm bright," the leader stepped around.

"Sharp, too, I notice."

"Yah. I eat razor soup."

"Well, however much of a soup eater you are, Jimmy, be mighty careful what you take out of that spring. For we know that the hunchback died. And who can say that he didn't drown in the spring while diving for the sunken treasure? And that being the case the spring naturally is haunted. Without a hoot-nannie, to protect you. you're liable to get teeth marks in your gizzard. For ghosts are crazy over gizzards. Some ghosts eat nothing else. I know that to be a fact, for I looked it up in the dream book.''

''Of all the crazy junk!''

''Then you don't believe in ghosts, huh?''

''*Me?* I should say not.''

''Well, Jimmy, I'll always be glad that I warned you. For you have a sweet smile.''

''You're funny.''

''I know it,'' came the modest admission. ''I was born that way. It's a sort of gift.''

Here Chet Milden tumbled into camp.

''There's a man at the spring,'' he panted.

''A man?'' Jimmy showed surprise.

''I saw him. Then he sort of vanished. And he had a hump on his back.''

Gee-miny crickets! What strange co-incidence was this? A hunchback! Who was he? And what was he doing here?

Jimmy's eyes quickly sought Scoop's.

''Did you hear that?'' he gasped.

''Sure thing,'' our resourceful leader quickly took advantage of the amazing situation. ''It's *him*, all right. I just got through telling you that the spring is haunted. And I pity you, kid,'' came the final solemn warning, ''if you touch that treasure.''

CHAPTER XI

OUR CLEVER ESCAPE

THE Tutter slaughter house is owned by a hunchback. And if you can find a kinder man than old Mr. Robbins I'd like to meet him. A friend of all boys, and sensibly interested in the things that boys are interested in, as all right-minded men should be, we hardly ever stop at his place to talk with him but what he lugs out an old skull as a present for one of us or gives us something else equally nice. Very often he gives us candy. So, as you can imagine, we think a great deal of him.

And through our association with him, both at the slaughter house and in his own home, where one spring we helped him paper the kitchen ceiling (which was the time Red sat down in the paste), we have come to realize that hunchbacks, as a rule, the same as other men, are fair and trustworthy. Once in a while you'll find a bad one, like the one from whom the silver was hidden, but not very often. So when Chet Milden rushed into camp, with the exciting story that he had just seen a strange hunchback at the spring, we weren't particularly scared.

Yet, what an amazing coincidence. If we had framed up the whole thing, story and all, the man's appearance on the scene couldn't have been timed more perfectly.

Plainly a kind Providence, now determined to favor us, had sent him here to help us. More than that, this same Providence, to a plan unknown to us in the beginning, and entirely unsuspected by us, had started Scoop off on the crazy "hoot-nannie" story. For without the story the hunchback's unexpected appearance at the spring wouldn't have materially helped us. You can figure that out.

As it was, Jimmy Stricker was dead sure that the spring was haunted. Not that he had completely swallowed our leader's silly "hoot-nannie" story. But here was proof! One of his own men had actually seen the deformed ghost. There could be no doubt.

So Jimmy promptly gave up all thought of lifting the treasure. For he had no desire to get in bad with a ghost, least of all a hunch-backed ghost of evil reputation. Oh, gee! You can't imagine how happy and heartened we were in the changed situation, even though my legs were all bit up by mosquitoes and Peg's nose, where he had gotten it in the soup, was

peeling. We still had a chance. As I say,
Fortune was favoring us.

But who was this unknown benefactor of
ours? That was the big puzzle to us. It was
well for our interests to encourage Jimmy in
his belief that the spring was haunted. But
we knew better. Chet had seen a man, not a
ghost. And the mere fact that the man had
"vanished," thus bearing out the "ghost"
theory, was unimportant. He probably didn't
want any of us to know that he was on the
island. That is why he had "vanished."

But what was he doing here? His actions
were mysterious. Could it be that he, too, knew
about the treasure in the spring? And had he
been detected in the act of looking the ground
over, with plans for early work? We hoped,
of course, that he didn't know the truth about
the spring. For it would be an unfortunate
situation for us to have a man working against
us, as well as Bid and his gang.

So, curious about the stranger, and now
somewhat doubtful, we were glad when Jimmy,
after guarded investigations at the spring, ordered his men to spread out and search the
island. I don't know what his idea was. But
we told him that it was a good idea. We even
begged him to untie us so that we, too, could
join in the important search. But he wasn't

quite dumb enough to fall for that. Bid would
soon be back, he said. And we could talk to
him instead.

Not only did the uneasy leader's scouts bring
back word that the island was completely deserted, except for ourselves, but it was their
further report that no boat of any kind had
been sighted in the surrounding lake. Added
proof, of course, in Jimmy's mind, that the
hunchback was indeed a ghost!

We let on that we were scared. For it was
to our interests to keep the others thinking that
some fearful unearthly peril hung over the
island—a peril, you might say, that had its
beginning in the murder of an old woman, such
being Jimmy's belief. Yet, knowing how widely
the others had missed the mark, we had a good
laugh at them behind their backs. The big
boobs!

Could it be, we then asked ourselves, turning
the matter around in our minds, that the mysterious hunchback, better informed on the
island's secret places than the others, was now
hiding in our big cave?

That wasn't impossible. In fact, as Scoop
contended, in further earnest consideration of
the matter, it was very probable. For where
else could the man be? So, more than ever
we wondered who he was. And we wondered,

too, kind of disappointed-like, how he had penetrated our secret. For, as I have written down,
we had told nobody about the new cave except
our parents and the island's new owner.

Jimmy stationed a weak-kneed sentinel near
the spring. But nothing more was seen of the
ghost. However, as we told the disturbed
leader, that was to be expected. For ghosts
rarely came out twice in the same day. In
fact, they seldom came out once unless it was
to give warning. So, to the safety of all of us,
it was well, we said, for the others to remember
what had happened.

Later Jimmy and Hib rowed out to the scow,
now anchored in the bay off the island's sandy
south shore. And during the time that they
were trying out their mechanical talents on the
balky motor the sun climbed higher and higher
in the summer sky. Another swell day. But
it meant nothing to us. At eleven-thirty Jimmy
yelled back to shore, telling Chet to get busy
and peel the spuds for dinner. Nor could our
lazy guard escape this hated task. For the
other two kids who were on the island had
meandered off into the west swamp, or, as we
called it, Cat-tail Marsh, to hunt turtles.

And now let me tell you what a slick trick
we pulled on Chet. Oh, gee! The wonder is
that we succeeded. But luck was with us.

"Oof!" Scoop turned up his nose, as the unwilling potato peeler got to work. "I don't envy you your job."

"Aw, shut up."

"Slavery."

"SHUT UP."

"And how unfair, too. For a fellow with your artistic touch ought to be carving statues instead of potatoes."

"Isn't he cruel!" Red watched the potato peeler. "He jabs the poor little spuds right in the eyes."

"Who wouldn't jab 'em in the eyes? Potato peeling! Oof! I'm glad I don't have to do it."

"And such a big panful, too. I bet it takes him till noon."

"Notice, though, how artistically he holds the knife."

"A mark of genius, kid. It's in him."

"Genius is right. And to think that his talents should be so wasted on mere potatoes! Sad, sad."

"Still, I heard that the man who carved the Statue of Liberty started in on potatoes. So, take heart, kid. Who knows but what you, too, will be a famous sculptor some day. And we'll be able to tell with pride that we watched you get your start—in a pan of potatoes."

"Say, you big fat-heads," the furious potato peeler boiled over. "I'll put a dent in somebody's mug, if you don't dry up."

"Honest, Chet, we enjoy watching you. There's something about your touch that— that— Well, kid, words can't express it."

"Oh-h-h-h!" Red then sucked in his breath, like a gurgling pump. "Did you see that? The knife slipped."

"My fist is going to slip, in about two jerks of a lamb's tail."

"Did you cut your little finger?"

"SHUT UP."

Scoop then told how an uncle of his, in the army, used to make the German prisoners peel the potatoes.

"That was a bright one," Red glared at the crafty leader. "Why don't you *ask* for the job, and have done with it?"

Listening with wide-open ears, Chet, big dumb-bell that he was, swallowed the bait, as you might say, hook, line and sinker. Oh, gee! Can you imagine? Having the authority of a guard, and wanting to turn the tables on us to thus pay us back for our smart talk, as well as to escape the hated job himself, he actually untied Scoop's hand and put the latter to work with a paring knife. A *knife,* mind you. That shows you how little the Strickers know. For Chet, of course, is representative of the gang that he chums around with.

Well, you can readily imagine what followed. There was a sudden wild squawk from the outwitted guard. And when he finally got the potato peelings out of his eyes, Scoop having pitched the whole mess into his face, dirty water and all, the camp's five prisoners, cut loose by their clever chum, were streaking it for the raft on the other side of the island.

"Hel-lp!" bawled Chet, thus attracting his leader's attention.

"What's the matter?" Jimmy bellowed to shore.

"They're gone."

"Who?"

"The prisoners. They just got away."

The leader let out a howl that carried for a mile.

"Oh, you dumb-dora! What Bid will do to you! I have a notion to sock you myself. Why in time didn't you watch them?"

"I did."

"Yah, I *bet* you did. Well, kid, you've got something coming when Bid gets here. I sure pity you."

"Oh, gee," Chet suffered in advance. "I couldn't help it."

By this time we had reached the raft, which, fortunately for us, hadn't been disturbed. And ten minutes later we were well on our way across the wide waters, the island behind us ringing with the cries of Jimmy and his gang as they followed us to the shore.

Stopping to swab his dripping face, Peg looked at us with a pair of grimly pleased eyes.

"And now," he gritted, eager for battle, as is his nature, "let's get Big Bertha tuned up and show them what five pirates can do."

Oh, gee! The fun that was coming! I could hardly wait.

CHAPTER XII

THE FEARFUL FIVE

IT was our plan now, as pirates, armed with a rusted pirate cutlass and dressed up in real pirate clothes, as provided for our use by the mystery trunk, to capture the scow, force the conquered enemy to walk the plank, in true pirate style, and then take undisputed possession of the island.

Of course, we didn't intend to actually *drown* the Strickers, or anything like that. As a matter of fact, so far as making them walk the plank was concerned, there wasn't a place in the wide waters, outside of the channel itself, clear over by the south shore, where the water was over their heads. So, even if we decided to confiscate their rowboat, they'd be able to wade to the mainland. Or, if they got stuck in the mud (and how funny that would be!), we could rescue them temporarily and then make them walk the plank again, for our further entertainment.

This was to be their pay for butting in on us. The smart alecks! And to think that they actually had tried to steal the treasure on us.

Gr-r-r-r! That's the way we felt now. Ready to fight to a finish. Our only regret was that Bid wouldn't be there to walk the plank with the rest of his scurvy gang. For he's the meanest one of the whole shooting-match. Why, even now, as you know, he was on his way to Tutter to sell the silver plate that we had fished out of the spring. And if that isn't downright stealing I don't know what is. He would have had a right to it if he had found it himself. But he hadn't. *We* had found it. So it was ours, not his. He had no right to it at all.

Knowing how eager Mrs. Dexter was to get her hands on old dishes, regardless of the cost, we could not doubt that she would jump at the chance of buying the silver plate, particularly when she learned that it was a part of the historic King's Silver. She'd never suspect, of course, that Bid had stolen the dish from us. For he would make up a likely story, leaving us out of the picture altogether. He's good at that kind of stuff. And so very probably he would receive the money that belonged to us.

Oh, if only we could get our mitts on him before he spent the money or turned it over to his parents. One time he and Jimmy caught me in a lonely alley and stood me on my head, keeping the marbles that they shook out of my pockets. Now I wanted to do the same to him.

And that is what we would do, Peg said grimly,
if we caught him—only, of course, what we
would shake out of the captured one's pockets,
instead of marbles, as in my case, would be
silver dollars and half dollars and quarters.
Or, to be more exact, *our* silver dollars and
half dollars and quarters. Right down to the
last penny.

As for the mysterious hunchback, if he were
indeed hiding in our big cave, as we still suspected, it would be an easy matter for us to
spot him. And by watching him on the sly we
probably would be able to learn his secret. In
case he knew nothing about the treasure, but
had come to the island for some other hidden
purpose, we would then secretly lift the complete treasure and rush it to town for safe-
keeping. Or, if we felt, after careful investigation, that he stood in our way, we could set
a trap for him and take him prisoner. That
may sound big to you. But you must remember
that there were five of us to his one. And
though separately we were much the smaller,
combined we probably had him outweighed
three to one. Besides, his capture would fur-
nish added excitement. And whoever heard of
a real treasure hunt that wasn't exciting! As
Scoop said, the more exciting the better. Absolutely, and nothing else but.

Old Chris was waiting for us at Tavern Beach. And as we landed on the sandy shore he whinnied happily. But we were too busy to give him much attention. And as we separated for quick work he followed first one active group and then the other with mournful, puzzled eyes, unable to figure out, I guess, why we didn't make the usual fuss over him.

Scoop had earlier brought in a crotch for our big slingshot. And as Peg had picked up an old leather boot, the upper part of which was suitable for a pouch, it took us not more than thirty minutes to complete and mount our "young cannon," as we now laughingly called it, on our raft. Also we put up a pole for our pirate flag. Red and Al were busy making clay balls, of which, when I called them to dinner, they had a pile two feet high. Some of this "ammunition" was hard, having been left in the sun from the preceding day. So, as Peg said, as we stowed away the hastily prepared noonday meal, if we failed to lay the enemy out with the soft "cannon balls," we could try a few of the hard ones.

"If only we could save the hard ones for Bid," I spoke up.

"That *would* be fun," Peg agreed. "Still," he considered, with a sandwich in one hand and a piece of pie in the other, "the loss of the treasure will hurt him a whole lot more than clay cannon balls. For I know that kid.''

''What do you suppose he'll do to Chet?'' said Red, thinking of our recent escape.

''Oh, he'll be plenty rough. There's no doubt about that. But Chet joined the gang of his own accord. So, having picked that kind of company, it's up to him to take his own medicine.''

''They sure are hard-boiled,'' laughed Scoop.

''How about us?'' grinned Red, looking ahead. ''Pirates are hard-boiled, too.''

With dinner out of the way, and our stuff gathered up for hasty removal to the island later on, we put in a half hour at target practice. And was Peg ever *good!* Toward the end of the practice period he got so he could put the ''cannon balls'' just where he wanted them. The enemy was doomed. There was no doubt about that.

Everything now made ready for the big battle so far as our armored craft was concerned, we ran back to the tavern, in final preparation, to get into our pirate clothes. Peg claimed the only pair of old-fashioned black buckled shoes that the trunk contained. Further, with our help, he dressed himself in a pair of baggy red bloomers, which came to his knees, and below which he let his stockings hang down, thus showing several inches of bare skin. One knee of the bloomers was patched with a piece of red-and-white tablecloth, or some such checkered material. With a black sash for a belt, and wearing a ragged shirt, the red and white stripes of which ran crosswise, like a convict's suit, he sure looked the part of a real pirate. He carried the rusted cutlass thrust into his sash, the knotted ends of which hung below his hips, and his arms were completely bare, on one of which we faked a tattoo design showing a red heart and a red anchor, Al having supplied the necessary colored ink. For a cap the chief gunner, as we now called him, wore a red and white polka-dot handkerchief, tied behind in a fancy knot, the ends hanging down almost to his belt. Then, as a final touch, we tied the big brass rings to his ears.

I came next, picking out a ragged black suit that was seventeen sizes too big for me. I can't imagine where it came from, or who had worn it ahead of the dead pirate, but such law breakers, I guess, pick up their loot everywhere. The ragged sleeves of my shirt came only to the elbows, and for effect the others bound one of my wrists with a handkerchief, splotched with red ink. A red scarf was then tied around my throat, the ends hanging down, one in front of my shoulder and the other behind. My "cap"

was a mate to Peg's, only the cloth was striped.
And to further make it appear that I had been
hacked up in some recent bloody battle, the
others decorated one of my cheeks with a fake
scar covered with court-plaster taken from our
first-aid kit.

Scoop had on a red shirt, the sleeves of which
came to his wrists, over which he wore a fancy
black vest. His pants were somewhat like
Peg's. Picking out a stocking cap, which had
a big red tassel, he wore this cap hanging down
on one ear, reminding me for all the world of
pictures that I had seen of Simple Simon.

Red and Al wore white shirts, splotched up
here and there with red ink. Each had a "General Washington" hat. To tell the truth I don't
remember what else they wore. But take it
from me they were fixed up *right*. Nothing in
the trunk was overlooked, except a set of false
teeth. Our only regret was that we hadn't a
cutlass apiece.

Now that we were real pirates, Peg said,
swaggering around in his patched bloomers, the
proper thing for us to do, before starting out
on our first blood-spilling expedition, was to
sing an appropriate pirate song. So we sang
the rollicking song about "Fifteen men on a
dead man's chest—yo-ho-ho and a bottle of
rum!" You should have heard us. Did we

ever make that old tavern ring! No wonder a
big chunk of plaster came tumbling down. But
it fell on Red, so we didn't care. Then Scoop
squared his shoulders and sang a new pirate
song that he had learned. Here it is:

O, my name was Captain Kidd, as I sailed, as I
    sailed,
O, my name was Captain Kidd, as I sailed;
My sinful footsteps slid, God's laws they did forbid,
But wickedly I did, as I sailed.

I saw three ships of France, as I sailed, as I sailed,
I saw three ships of France, as I sailed,
I saw three ships of France, to them I did advance,
I took 'em all by chance, as I sailed.

I saw three ships of Spain, as I sailed, as I sailed,
I saw three ships of Spain, as I sailed,
I saw three ships of Spain, I fired on 'em amain,
Till most of 'em were slain, as I sailed.

I knifed brave Willie Moore, as I sailed, as I sailed,
I knifed brave Willie Moore, as I sailed,
I knifed brave Willie Moore, and I left him in his
    gore,
Not many leagues from shore, as I sailed.

With ninety bars of gold, as I sailed, as I sailed,
With ninety bars of gold, as I sailed,
With dollars manifold, and riches all untold,
And so I lost my soul, as I sailed.

That was a peachy song, we said, bragging
on the leader. But when we asked him to teach
it to us, so that we could sing it, too, Peg started

us off toward the raft, unwilling to longer delay the attack.

So, with reckless, dare-devil hearts, as you might say—with our pirate flag flying in the summer breeze and a doughty pirate song on our lips, the Fearful Five, as we now called ourselves, set forth in battle trim, four of us poling and the fifth steering. And how big and strong I felt in that pirate suit! Gee-miny crickets! I could have strangled a full-grown lion just as easy as pie. Nor was it hard for me to further imagine, as I jiggled my pole around in the mud, that behind me lay a long trail of blood and outlawry. Dead-eye Dave the demon of the desert. That was me, all right. Miserly country squires who foreclosed mort-gages on defenseless widows, like in the Alger books, trembled at mention of my name. Yet the poor and needy loved me for the gallant knight of the highway that I was. Still, I con-sidered, kind of proud of the way I was helping the poor and needy, I couldn't very well be the demon of the desert if I were a pirate. For pirates did their pirating on the ocean. So a more suitable name probably would be Wall-eyed Walt the wicked wizard of the waltzing waves. Or possibly Buzzard Bill the bloody butcher of the bounding billows. I'm real good at thinking up names like that.

Loaded down as we were with extra clothes, it was blamed hot work pushing that old raft along. Yet nobody complained, least of all Wall-eyed Walt, etc., etc. For, as I say, we liked this idea of being dressed up for the occasion. It gave us added courage. Besides, think of the reward that lay ahead of us. A treasure worth thousands of dollars.

With a hundred silver dishes, as we sailed, as we
        sailed,
With a hundred silver dishes, as we sailed,
With silver manifold, and riches all untold,
And so we lost our souls, as we sailed.

We knew this verse now. And did we ever yip it out, changing the bars of gold to silver dishes, and so on. Oh, baby! Talk about your real *fun*.

The Strickers heard us coming. And I dare say that after one good look at us, bloodthirsty cutthroats that we appeared to be, they were scared out of their wits. Anyway, Jimmy promptly ordered the tents pulled down and loaded on the scow, the motor of which was again in running order.

Swinging around the west end of the island, dripping wet from our hard work but with buoyant hearts, we sought to head them off, realizing that if they once got into the channel it would be a hopeless task for us to try and overtake them. For our raft had no speed at all.

But again luck favored us. And did we ever yip with joy when that lovely, beautiful, magnificent motor of ours died on them in characteristic style almost as soon as they got started. Sweet doctor! Our fun was assured. For the only course now left open to them, cowards that they appeared to be, was to stay and fight. And that is exactly what we wanted.

Jimmy had yelled at us in derision when they started off, the front deck of the scow loaded high with their stuff and the single rowboat trailing behind. He thought, of course, that he was going to make a sure get-away. But he was yelling a different kind of a yell now.

"You've *got* to start it," he hung over Hib, who was cranking his head off.

"I can't," the engineer sweat.

"Turn on the gasoline."

"I did turn it on."

"And the switch, too?"

"Of course. Do you think I'm dumb enough to do all this cranking with the gas and juice shut off?"

"It wouldn't be anything surprising," grunted Jimmy, remembering what had happened on the island that morning, "if you take after your brother."

"The motor's nothing but an old junk-pile, anyway," Hib gave the balance wheel a kick.

"Don't be dumb. Instead of kicking it, try and find out what's the matter with it."

Chet Milden had been watching us over the gunwale.

"Look at 'em," he cried. "They've got a sword."

"Wood, I bet."

"Ho, ho, ho!" bellowed Peg, like a real pirate. "Wood, is it? You'll think differently, you bunch of cock-eyed bog jumpers, when we ram it through your homely gizzards."

"Say, who do you think you are?" Jimmy further sneered. "Captain Kidd?"

"Look us over, frog-face."

"I don't see much."

"The Fearful Five."

"Including Buzzard Bill the bloody butcher of the bounding billows," I put in.

"And Hack-'em-up Hank," Scoop gave himself a name in pattern of me. "The howling horror of the heaving horizon."

"What are you doing—putting on a program?"

"Oh, we just came over to play tiddledy winks with you. Didn't we, Peg?"

"Ho, ho, ho!" again roared old hefty. Then, bellowing orders, in full command, he had us swing about and steady the raft for the first broadside. Swish-h-h-h! went the clay ball through the air. Stooping over the motor, trying furiously to get it started, Hib got the soft "cannon ball" squarely in the seat of the pants. Over he went on his face, howling to beat the cars. Gee-miny crickets! I don't know whether real pirates, in a similar situation, would have laughed or not. But bu-lieve me *we* laughed.

It was Bid's big idea, we learned later, to make a gunboat of the old scow, which, he figured, would give him the same kind of protection on his appropriated island that a country's navy provides. So Jimmy, in deserting the island, had tried to save the scow for his leader's later use. But that important plan had miscarried. And now, as I say, the temporary leader, evidently less of a coward than we had suspected, seeing that it was a case of fight or surrender, grimly got down to business.

"We drove 'em away before," he bellowed encouragingly to his warriors. "And we can do it again. Out with your slingshots, gang. And use *pebbles* this time. Are you ready? One, two, three, *fire.*"

Al got a crack on the leg. But he didn't whimper. Nor did Buzzard Bill, who received one in the bread-basket. And then "Big

Bertha'' got in another shot, failing, however,
to do any personal damage this time.

And so we fought back and forth, first one
side scoring a hit and then the other. We
didn't dare close in on them. For at closer
range they might have put out an eye for us.
A fellow has to think of those things. As Dad
says, it's all right for boys to have fun, even
rough fun like this, but no one but a reckless
dumb-bell would run the needless chance of
losing an eye or an ear.

The trouble was, as we now saw, that they
could get in ten shots to our one. What we
needed was a slingshot apiece. Moreover, we
needed some kind of a shield. For the only
protection we had was our thick clothing.

Still, we kept on as gritty as ever.
Swish-h-h-h! Peg's aim was almost perfect.
But the others, by watching him, knew just
when to duck behind the gunwale. So no damage was done, the ''cannon balls,'' for the most
part, squashing against the scow's plank sides
or on the deserted decks.

Probably, instead of carrying on the fight,
as described, the more sensible plan would have
been for us to forget about the Strickers, even
to the temporary loss of our scow, and proceed
to lift the treasure. But we wanted to show
Jimmy and his gang that we could lick them.

More than that, as pirates, we wanted to make them walk the plank. After all of our preparations and big talk it would have been galling to us to give up now. We simply wouldn't think of it for a single instant.

Peg was sweating like a butcher.

"Duck, you scum of the earth," he bellowed, letting fly.

"What are you aiming at?" jeered Jimmy. "The moon?"

"Shove up your head again, you short-eared jas-sack, and I'll show you what I'm aiming at."

"You couldn't hit the broad side of a barn."

"*Some* slingshot," another one of the smart alecks piped up.

Swish-h-h-h! went another "cannon ball."

"Missed us by a mile," Jimmy squawked triumphantly, as the charge squashed harmlessly against the heavy gunwale. "I told you that you couldn't aim straight. Why don't you try it backwards?"

"Or let Buzzard Bill shoot it for a change. He's funny."

Al looked worried.

"We aren't getting anywhere," he told the sweating gunner.

"Well," bellowed Peg, all worked up, "if you think your aim is any better than mine, hop to it."

"I didn't mean that," Al flushed.

"Get out of my way," the big one then ordered roughly. "I'll sock 'em this time. Watch me."

But again he failed to do any damage.

It was then, as I recall, that Scoop, to our surprise, slid into the water and swam to the island.

"Don't let 'em get away," he shouted back to us, when he had waded ashore. "I'll be back in twenty minutes with some *real* ammunition."

Hearing this, and evidently getting cold feet, Jimmy promptly waved a white flag. Surprised at the unexpected surrender, we yelled to Scoop to come back. But he was out of hearing, having disappeared on the run in the direction of the big spring.

Jimmy's warriors all had their hands up. But this, we learned, was just a trick of theirs to get us within more telling range of their slingshots. Gee-miny crickets, did they ever pepper us. *Wough!*

And then, I suppose, is when we should have "rushed" them regardless, fighting it out, hand to hand, on their own deck, which is what real pirates would have done. In fact, Peg ordered full speed ahead. But we balked. It was too dangerous, we said, wanting to save our eyes and ears.

So, backing off, with not more than twenty "cannon balls" left, our only hope, seemingly, lay in Scoop.

Twenty minutes! That would be one shot a minute. But suppose the leader's plans, whatever they were, miscarried and he didn't get back for an hour or two? Gosh! Butcher Bill the buzzard of the bloody billows, or whatever it was, would feel real cute sneaking off to the island with his tail between his legs like a whipped puppy.

Pirates, I saw now, with considerable less enthusiasm, had a lot of ups and downs.

CHAPTER XIII

HOW WE WON THE BATTLE

Scoop is a smart kid. And, as a rule, as I have mentioned before, he makes a corking good leader. Of course, like everybody else, he has his faults. And still having a few things to learn, he blunders now and then. But that is nothing to hold against him. For his successes, as you might say, due to his clever ideas, far outnumber his failures.

So, having a great deal of faith in him, yet disappointed, in a way, that he hadn't taken us into his confidence, we set about to carry on the battle as instructed until he got back. About all we could do, though, outside of putting across an occasional shot, was to keep up a bold front, letting on, as blustering pirates, that things were working out to our complete satisfaction, which, as you know, wasn't the case at all. With our pirate rigging, and the big slingshot, we had counted on an easy victory. But, if anything, we had more sore spots than the enemy. For not only had they gotten in ten shots to our one, as I say, but their pebbles raised bigger welts than our clay balls. I

had one "knob" on my left leg that was a
beauty. And did I ever want to rub it! Gee-
miny crickets, how it smarted! But knowing
that the enemy was watching me I held off.
And so to them, from all outward appearances,
I was still Buzzard Bill the bloody butcher, etc.,
as blustering and as breezy as ever. Peg set
us this courageous example. And was he ever
good with his swaggering, swashbuckling "Ho,
ho, ho!" and "Haw, haw, haw!" stuff. It was
fun to pattern after him.

You never would have suspected from the
Strickers' chesty actions that earlier they had
tried to skin out with the scow to thus avoid
an open battle with us. Having successfully
held us off, they thought that they were the
whole works. There was a quick change in
them, however, and a sudden drying up of their
big talk, when, as has been described, Scoop
disappeared into the island on his mysterious
errand.

Something was going to happen. They realized that, all right. And fearing some kind of
a clever trap, in which they very probably
would get the worst of it, as had happened to
them before when our foxy leader limbered up
his wits, they decided to carry out their original plan and evaporate from the scene while
the evaporating was good.

So Hib was told to hurry up and jiggle the

motor into action. And when he politely declined to expose his precious carcass on the unprotected rear deck, where, as you'll remember, our "cannon" had earlier cracked him a neat one in the seat of the pants, the leader resourcefully had two of his warriors hold up a canvas strip, behind which the engineer hurriedly got to work with a screwdriver and the starting crank.

Nor could we drive them back to the pit. For our "cannon balls" did no harm, the stretched canvas acting as a sort of cushion. And when we changed the position of our raft, to get a possible crack at them from behind, they in turn neatly swung the scow around.

We could hear Hib cranking. And soon, to our disappointment, the motor relieved itself of a sickly puff.

"Hot dog!" yipped the engineer. "Did you hear that, Jimmy?"

"She's coming. Twist her again, Hib. Atta-boy! There she goes! We'll get away from here after all."

Peg was crazy.

"We've got to stop 'em, fellows," he panted. And then, grabbing the spare pole, he started pushing with all his might, which, to me, seemed like a useless effort. For the motor, after the usual preliminary coughing spell, was now running at fairly good speed.

There was a combined triumphant shout from the scow's rear deck as the heavy boat began to pull away from us.

"Look at 'em work," jeered the leader. "As though they could catch us now—the big simps."

"Push," panted Peg, like the dogged kid that he is. *"Push,* I tell you. The motor's missing again. Hear it? We can overtake 'em if we *work."*

Sure of their escape, however hard we were trying to overtake them, the others further jeered at us, calling us galley slaves.

"We'll never make it," I gasped, straining every muscle in my body.

"We've *got* to make it."

"And fight it out on their own deck?"

"Sure thing."

"But it's five to our four."

"I'll take three if you guys'll only take the other two."

And he meant it, too. Good old Peg! I never knew a grittier kid. He sure is a peach. Oh, gee! I wouldn't trade his close friendship for seven tons of gold. That's how much I appreciate *him.* And it makes me happy to know that he has the same warm feeling for me. Do you have a buddy like that? If not, I want to tell you that you're missing some of the finest joy in the world—the joy of true companionship.

As though to spite us, and do exactly what we didn't want it to do, the motor quickened its speed. So finally I threw down my pole in despair. It was no use, I told Peg, gasping for air. The scow was traveling twice as fast as us. We were just wasting our strength.

But would old hefty admit defeat? Not on your life. Grabbing two clay balls he rolled them into one. Then, aiming at the motor, he let fly.

Bing! Bending over the motor, oilcan in hand, Hib almost jumped out of his skin when the clay ball struck the spinning balance wheel.

"*Good* night!" he screeched, as the particles of clay flew in all directions. "He's trying to wreck his own motor."

"Yes," bellowed Jimmy, who readily got the drift of the gunner's scheme, "and you ought to know *why* he's trying to wreck it. But keep it a-going, Hib. And we'll tend to *him*."

Bing! This time the double charge of clay struck the carburetor.

"Out with your slingshots and drive 'em back," Jimmy bellowed to his warriors, as the motor began to gag, evidently having swallowed more clay than was good for it. "Are you ready? One, two, three, *fire*."

At the final word we turned our backs, getting the charge, for the most part, in the seat of our pants, which, as you can imagine, considering how close we were to the shooters, and how tight our pants were, wasn't very pleasant for us. Still, as we all agreed, it was better to back up to it than to face it. Then, wheeling and working quickly, Peg socked another charge into the limping motor.

"Hurray!" screeched Red, jumping with joy. "You got 'er that time, old kid."

"Yes," bellowed Jimmy, furious over our success in stalling the motor, "and we're going to get you, too, you frog-eyed doughnut. Take that," he let fly, "and see how you like it."

"Ouch!" squawked Red, as the pebble struck him in the stomach.

"Made you smart, huh?"

"Boy, your nose'll smart if I ever get a crack at it."

"Come on and do it now," the dare was then thrown out to us. "You'll never get a better chance."

"Sure thing," Chet swaggered back and forth. "Why don't you come ahead, as you said, and fight us on our own deck? We're all ready for you."

"And they call themselves pirates," jeered Hib, when we made no move to accept their dare.

"Hack-'em-up Hank and Buzzard Bill," another ridiculed.

"They're yellow. They don't dare to attack us."

"*Pirates!* Haw, haw, haw! They'd make good ribbon clerks."

"Or dressmakers."

"Sewing lace on petticoats, huh?"

"I bet mamma washes their ears for them."

This was all done to sort of coax us on, so that they could get a better crack at us with their slingshots. But we weren't dumb. And at Peg's sensible orders we quickly backed off.

Hib reported to Jimmy that our last shot had wrecked the timer. It was useless, the engineer declared, to continue cranking.

"But what are we going to do?" Jimmy bawled helplessly. "We can't hold out forever."

"Let 'em have their old scow. It's nothing but junk, anyway."

They talked this over.

"Hot puppy!" cried Red, as the others came to a decision. "They're getting ready to start out in the rowboat."

Jimmy, though, contrary to our hopes, was too wise to overload the rowboat, realizing the predicament that he and the others would be in if the boat began dipping water. Ordering two of his men into the boat, he started them off with the camping stuff, instructing the rower to come back with the empty boat, after which, of course, it was the intention of the others to kiss the old scow good-by.

Nor could we do anything to upset these plans. For the rowboat had double our speed. And though the scow's fighting force was now reduced to three, one less than our force, armed as they were with slingshots they still had the advantage of us.

We had been too busy to give much thought to Scoop, or to speculate on what he was doing or what was keeping him. But now to our great joy, just when we needed him the most, he came into sight in the water-logged skiff off the island's west end.

There was that in the rower's long, powerful strokes that told of success. He had set out to do something. And he had done it. Jimmy almost had a fit.

"Hurry," he screeched to his own returning oarsman.

Pulling alongside, Scoop, with a big grin, handed us a pailful of clay balls, which in themselves proved to us that after picking up the skiff on the island, where he and I had left it the night of the attack at the spring, he had rowed to Tavern Beach, later following the most direct course from there to the raft.

"Handle 'em carefully," he told us, referring to the clay balls.

"Why?" Peg inquired, looking curiously into the pail. "Are they loaded with gunpowder?"

"Even worse than that," grinned Scoop, "they're loaded with rotten eggs."

"*What?*" stared old hefty.

"I saw the nest of eggs the other day when I was picking berries. Some hen from Cadman's farmhouse, I guess. But I never dreamed that the eggs would come in handy."

Peg's face glowed with a new joy.

"*Rotten eggs,*" he cried. "Oh, baby!"

"I broke one by accident," Scoop went on. "But bu-lieve me I didn't stick around *there* very long. I guess not. For the stink almost strangled me."

It is possible that you never have had any experience with rotten eggs. So, for your information, I'll add here that they are the stinkingest things imaginable.

"*Rotten eggs,*" Peg cried again, with dancing eyes. "Scoop, if your face wasn't so dirty I'd reward you with a kiss. How in the world did you ever think of it?"

"*Me?* Oh," the leader continued his broad grin, "I think of a lot of things. . . . Anything happen while I was away?"

"I'll tell the world," piped up Red, eager to recite his tale of woe. "Jimmy Stricker shot me right in the stomach. And when I get hold of him I'm going to push his face clear through the back of his head."

There were sharp ears on the scow.

"What?" jeered the opposing leader. "A little shrimp like you? Don't make me laugh."

"*Laugh?*" bellowed Red. "Say, kid, you'll weep sackcloth and ashes, or whatever it is, before I get through with you."

"Poodle-face."

"Yah, and you'll get another crack for that, too."

The situation on the scow having been further explained to our returned chum, we then got ready for business. And as soon as the rowboat touched the side of the scow, where Jimmy and the other two kids were waiting on needles and pins, notwithstanding the leader's smart talk to Red, we let fly, Peg, of course, acting as gunner.

"Oh, my gosh!" squawked Jimmy, as the over-ripe hen fruit began to smash around him. "They're shooting rotten eggs at us."

"*Rotten eggs!*" another kid bellowed in pattern.

"Quit shoving me—I don't want to get hit."

"You shoved me first."

"Oh, oh, oh! Now look at me."

"Give me AIR. I'm strangling."

And so they kept it up. Talk about a *stink*.

It was sickening to us. So how much worse must it have been for them.

In the excitement the rowboat got loose and drifted off. So, one after another, they plunged into the lake, clothes and all, which I'll have to admit is as close as we came that trip to making them walk the plank.

But did we kick? Hardly. Instead of going on board to dish out further punishment to them, as planned, we were only too glad to keep a healthy distance from the stinking old scow.

As for the others, after floundering around in the muddy water, like a lot of walruses, up-setting the boat two or three times, they finally managed to get away, the stinkingest, wettest, muddiest and maddest bunch of kids that I ever saw in all my life.

And so the scow was ours. Likewise the island and the treasure. Our victory, as pirates, was complete.

CHAPTER XIV

THE SEALED CAVERN

PEG, in continued blustering command, told us that we were as gallant a crew of rum-soaked cutthroats as ever graced the slippery poop deck of a pirate frigate, which, of course, was stuff fitting the occasion that he had picked up in a book.

"Blood!" he further bellowed, carving a hunk out of the air with his wicked cutlass. "The deck of our noble ship is drenched with the gore of our butchered enemies. So lift up your scarred faces in a smug smile, my bleary-eyed beauties. For at last we are avenged. Ah-HA-A-A-A-A! We are indeed avenged."

After which clever little oration he gruffly ordered us to fall into line for roll call.

"Buzzard Bill the bloody butcher of the bounding billows," Scoop read through his nose, pretending that he had an open book in his hands.

Which, of course, was me. So after a neat little buck-and-wing dance I gave the proper salute.

"Aye, aye, sir," I posed.

"Dusty Dan the daring demon of the deep."

"Aye, aye, sir," Al jigged and saluted in pattern.

"Wall-eyed Willie the wicked weasel of the wharves."

"Aye, aye, sir," grinned Red, showing what he could do.

"Hack-'em-up Hank the howling horror of the horizon."

"Present," the scowling captain spoke gruffly for the leader, who, not to be outdone by the rest of us, took time away from his job to reel off a few fancy dance steps of his own.

"Cap'n Kidd," the final name was then read off.

"Present," again spoke the gruff voice.

"Your orders have been obeyed, Cap'n."

"And what are our losses?"

"None at all, sir. Our crew is complete to the last man."

"And a fine crew it is," the pleased captain then looked us over with approving eyes, as he swaggered back and forth in front of us. "It's glad I am, my men, that you're all on deck to answer to your names. And for this splendid day's work, my hearties, you shall have your just reward. A quarter of the loot is yours."

"Hurray!" we yipped at the top of our voices.

"Mind you, though, no personal killing to get a bigger share. I'll have none of that."

"And the rum, Cap'n?" Scoop inquired, in pretended eagerness. "How about the rum?"

"A double portion for every man jack of you, black-hearted sea dogs that you are."

"Hurray!" we chorused again.

"No, not a double portion," the captain further swaggered, "but a *triple* portion. For may it never be said against me, when I have passed on to Davey Jones, that I was not at all times a generous provider as well as a fearless leader."

"HURRAY!" we fairly raised the sky.

"And now, my brave scallawags, let's away to yon desert isle to bury our loot."

"Aye, aye, Cap'n."

"Out with the treasure chests. One for you, as I so nobly said, and three for me."

"Aye, aye, Cap'n."

"And if there's one among you with sticky fingers—off goes his head. For I'll have no cheating on board this ship. We're an honest crew. If there's any cheating to be done I'll do it myself."

"Aye, aye, Cap'n. You can trust us. We're honorable men."

"Thieving, lying curs—that's what you are."

"Aye, aye, Cap'n. As you will."

"Cutthroats and robbers."

"Aye, aye, Cap'n. You must have your little joke."

"But, as I said before, you're a crew after my own heart."

"Aye, aye, Cap'n."

"I picked you one and all. And I picked well."

"Aye, aye, sir."

"And now, my hearties," old hefty further beamed at us, as he pulled up his sagging bloomers, "let's have a little song. A jolly old sea chantey. *Come!* Oil up your cracked voices with another scuttle of rum and join in. Everybody now. *Sing,* I tell you. Sing, or by the frozen soul of poor Willie Moore I'll sliver your bloomin' heads with my cudgel."

And sing we did!

Fifteen men on the dead man's chest—
  Yo-ho-ho and a bottle of rum!
Drink and the devil had done for the rest—
  Yo-ho-ho and a bottle of .um!
The mate was fixed by the bos'n's pike,
The bos'n brained with a marlinspike,
And Cookey's throat was marked belike,
    It had been gripped
    By fingers ten,
    And there they lay,
    All good dead men,
Like break o' day in a booking ken—
  Yo-ho-ho and a bottle of rum!

Boy, that sure was great!

Across the lake young "stink-foot" and his gang had landed on the main shore close to the channel. And now we could see their washed clothes swinging on a line stretched in the hot sun between two huge willow trees.

Which sort of drew our attention to the unpleasant fact that the rotten-egg smell had gotten into our own clothes more or less. Phew! I almost lost my dinner. So, in pattern of the others, after towing our stinking scow to a safe anchorage in the shallow shaded bay and further drawing our raft onto the sandy beach, we stripped to the bare skin and put on a neat little open-air lavatory stunt of our own.

That was one time, I'll admit, when it was a real pleasure to use soap. Boy, did we ever scrub ourselves. And did the water ever feel good to our heated bodies. Later we chucked our pirate clothes into a hollow tree, hoping that by the time we needed them again they'd be nicely aired out.

And so that part of our fun was over for the present.

It was important, Scoop said, in planning things, to get the island in shape for a possible siege before Bid Stricker got back. So he and I rowed back to the tavern for our supplies

"*ROTTEN EGGS*" ANOTHER KID BELLOWED.

Jerry Todd Pirate.

Page 162

while the others went off briskly in the direction of the big cave, hoping, as detectives, to quickly clear up the mystery of the peculiar-acting hunchback, after which, of course, if everything was safe, it was our further plan to lift the treasure and speed it away to a place of safety.

Finding our stuff unmolested we quickly loaded it into the skiff and started back to the island where Peg met us on the beach with the amazing report that the hunchback had sealed himself in the big cave.

"The hole that you fellows made in the wall behind the cupboard is entirely sealed up again," we were told.

"But what makes you think that the hunchback is in the cave?" Scoop inquired, in growing amazement.

"Where else can he be? It's the only hiding place on the island. You know that. Besides, the wall, with its fresh mortar, has every appearance of having been built from the inside."

"Well, I'll be jiggered," cried Scoop.

With further reference to the "Whispering Cave" book, and to the walled-up doorway that we had discovered behind the Bible peddler's tall cupboard, you probably will recall that we had not the slightest idea at the time that this sealed passageway gave entrance to another and much bigger cave. What we had expected to find, in tearing the wall down, was a shallow recess, on the order of a closet—a sort of hidden money vault, as it were, or something like that. But instead, as mentioned, we had tapped a vast network of caverns, the main corridor of which sloped down to a big silent pool, black and mysterious, which apparently was fed by the canal through a subterranean tunnel.

"Maybe the hunchback and the Bible peddler are in cahoots," was the theory I then shoved out, as Scoop's bewilderment continued.

"What do you mean?"

"They had a *reason* for sealing up the big cave. See? A very *important* reason. For instance," I drew on my imagination, "having worked the crooked Bible scheme together, they may have thousands of dollars hidden away in one of the secret chambers. Or they may be bank robbers as well as grafters. So, with one of them in jail—meaning old Joshua, of course—the other one came back to the cave to make sure that the money was safe. And finding a hole in the wall, where he didn't *want* a hole, he got busy and plugged it up, hoping to thus keep us out."

To all of which Scoop listened patiently but without comment.

Later we duplicated Jimmy Stricker's unsuccessful search of the island. Still, even if the hunchback *had* built the wall from the inside, as was our general belief, he wasn't necessarily a self-made prisoner. For there was another entrance. I mentioned this to Scoop. But the "window" in the east ravine, as discovered by us in our earlier explorations, a passageway for bats and owls, was found to be completely buried under a recent landslide.

Climbing around on the side of the steep hill, with changing theories, the excited leader then made the important discovery that a blast had been touched off just above the buried opening. Which was proof, he declared, that the complete closing up of the big cave was intentional.

What *could* be the cave's secret? Was it loot, as I had suggested? Or was it something more weird and sinister—something, possibly, dating back to the lifetime of the innkeeper and his wife?

There had been no sound of a local powder blast since our arrival in the neighborhood. So, in further discussion of the mystery, we were inclined to believe that the smaller entrance had been closed up several days ago. Yet the hunchback had peculiarly delayed sealing himself in until to-day. Had he, in the meantime, been living in the cave?

"It looks to me," reflected Scoop, as we

walked back to camp, where Peg and Red were getting supper, "as though there's something in the cave that the hunchback doesn't want us to see. It may be loot, as you say. Still, loot could be moved or easily covered up. So it must be something that is a *part* of the cave— something that can't be moved."

"But why should the man seal himself in?" I puzzled.

"I wish I knew," the other shrugged.

"He'll die," I shivered, "if he doesn't get fresh air."

"Maybe he wants to die."

"*Some* tomb," I further shivered, thinking of the vast cavern.

Mrs. Morrison, I had been told, was a "voodooer." Moreover, it was known throughout the neighborhood during her lifetime that she had a "secret reason" for refusing to let the island pass out of the family's immediate ownership. Could it be, I then wondered, as I walked along beside Scoop, hoping that Peg and Red wouldn't be stingy with the baked beans or get spiders in the soup, that the mystery of the cave had something to do with "voodooism"? For instance, was the hunchback a "voodooer," too? Did he share Mrs. Morrison's strange secret? And having survived her, was he now acting in the interests of that probable secret?

"Voodooism!" It had a queer dangerous sound. And how weird, too, that the old lady had been able to accurately predict her own death? Having this uncanny power, through her queer religion, it was barely possible that she might be able to "come back" after all.

Gee! I didn't like the thought of her coming back. That was too blamed spooky to suit me.

Stopping at the spring to get a drink we found Al poking around with the grab-pole, eager, of course, as the treasure's owner, to bring more of it to light. But he had nothing to show for his work.

A quicker and better plan of getting at the sunken treasure, we then agreed, was to drain the spring by tearing down its stone walls, as the Strickers had talked of doing. So we set to work, the three of us. And it was from this job that we later were called to supper.

Acting as chief waiter, Peg dished out the baked beans and other truck to us. And was that ever a grand and glorious meal! Oh, baby! I guess, though, that anything would have tasted good to us that night. For the battle had put an added edge on our appetites.

Later, with the exception of Red, who was

posted on the south shore to watch for Bid's expected return, we all went back to the spring, hoping that in the remaining two hours of daylight we'd be able to completely lift the treasure, after which, as mentioned, it was our plan to start off with it for Steam Corners or put it away in some other safe hiding place.

But to our disappointment and mounting bewilderment we found nothing in the drained spring except a dozen or more "hardheads." With the exception of the one plate, now in Bid's possession, the complete treasure had been mysteriously spirited away.

Mrs. Cassidy had said something about a *netik*—a sort of "voodoo" charm, as I understood it, having queer deadly powers. Could it be, I then explored my tangled wits for an answer to the riddle, that the King's Silver was a *netik?* Was that the reason why the hunchback, a probable "voodooer," himself, and thus informed on the secrets of the peculiar religion, had taken the silver into the cave with him, out of our reach? And by this act had he saved us from some unknown peril?

Queer thoughts, surely. But they matched the situation. Certainly, we knew that the hunchback was no ordinary treasure hunter. For if he had coveted the treasure, itself, he never would have sealed himself in the big cave.

Evidently Mrs. Morrison had known in her
later years that the silver was hidden in the
spring. That is why she had refused to sell the
island. The hunchback, too, whoever he was,
had peculiarly shared the old lady's knowledge
of the silver's hiding place. Yet neither of
them had dared to touch it during the owner's
lifetime. Nor had the hunchback dared to act
alone in its removal until this emergency arose.

Starting back to camp, empty-handed and
strangely disturbed, we ran into Red, who told
us that Bid Stricker was back in the wide
waters again.

"He's over there talking with Jimmy," the
sentinel reported. "And he's got a woman
with him."

CHAPTER XV

A DARING SCHEME

MRS. DEXTER had heard of the King's Silver through her mother. But she never had dreamed that it would be her good fortune to add this historic set to her already large dish collection until the day Bid Stricker unexpectedly breezed into her house with the recovered silver plate.

It was his story, of course, that *he* had found the dish in the big spring on Oak Island. And if the excited collector thought of us at all, as being in that neighborhood, it never had occurred to her that the dish had been stolen from us. For Bid very carefully made no mention of our names.

Acting promptly, to her own unique interests, she had set out for the island with the young treasure hunter, who, of course, was all het up over his easy success. Automobiles! Motor boats! Gumdrop factories! He could have them all. For when the silver had changed hands he would be as rich as Missouri mud.

But his castle of dreams took a complete

belly-flop, as you might say, when, after steady, hard rowing, he arrived in the wide waters. For there was his straggled gang waiting without purpose on the mainland. And what a sad, sad story they had to tell when he joined them! Much less than having lifted the treasure, as he had ordered, they had been driven from the "haunted" island with rotten eggs, the prisoners having made their escape shortly after the appearance of a hunchbacked "ghost."

The quarter-mile stretch of water between the island and the main shore acted as a sort of sounding board, like the head of a banjo, and at times, when the others were facing us, we could hear practically everything they said. Bid in particular, as the discomfiting story was dished out to him, bellowed like a suffering bull. And the only thing that saved Chet Milden's hide, I dare say, was the presence of Mrs. Dexter, who, listening in, stiffened with indignation when she learned the truth about the treasure.

It takes a woman to lay down the law to a fellow. And right then is when Bid got his. Oh, baby! I hope that no one ever tells me the things that Mrs. Dexter told him. Still, what else could he expect? A liar always gets caught that way.

Through with him for good and all, unprincipled cheat that he was, and anxious to get into decent company, she gave him the choice of rowing her to the island, where she had spotted us in a group on the shore, or giving up his boat. And though it galled him to knuckle down to her, as his actions showed, he very quickly came to a decision. For he saw plainly enough that she meant business.

"Hi, Mrs. Dexter," I shouted, as the rowboat pulled into our bay, the unwilling oarsman glowering at us over his shoulder.

This greeting brought a quick smile to the passenger's face.

"Hi, Jerry," she waved. "Any chance of getting overnight accommodations on this wonderful island of yours?"

"Sure thing," I grinned. "We have one room with running water—only the water is in the spring. And the spiders and mosquitoes have all been trained to sit back and look on."

"How splendid!" she laughed in her jolly way.

"You should have brought your mother along," I then told her, remembering how fond the old lady was of outdoor life.

"Indeed, she wanted to come the worst way. But I was afraid she might get excited and upset the boat."

"Huh!" grunted Bid, who had been taking in the conversation with a sullen face. "I'm blamed glad you didn't bring her."

"What's the matter, dearie?" purred Peg, waiting at the edge of the water. "Are your little arms getting tired?"

"Aw, shut up. I didn't come here to chin with you."

"You should have been here this afternoon, Bid," Peg added brightly. "We had a *wonderful* time. Didn't we, gang?"

"I'll tell the world," laughed Scoop.

"Huh!"

"Rotten eggs and everything."

"SHUT UP, I tell you."

"Makes you feel kind of neglected, huh? Well, you needn't. For we're saving two big goose eggs for you."

"*Goose* eggs," Red wedged in his bazzoo. "*Goose* eggs for a *goose!* That's a good one. Haw, haw, haw!"

Bid's eyes uneasily searched our hands.

"Say. . . . If you guys dare to paste me with a rotten egg I'll murder the whole outfit."

"Honest?" Peg continued his sweet smile

"You heard what I said."

"Suppose, then, being our company, we kiss you, instead."

"You aren't funny."

"We mustn't do that either, huh?"

"Try it once and see what you get."

"All right, Bid," laughed Peg. "You're safe."

"Why do you say that?" Red showed disappointment. "I thought we were going to sock him with rotten goose eggs."

"To-morrow," grinned Peg.

"But why not now?" the smaller one hung on.

"And run the chance of hitting Mrs. Dexter? Don't be dumb. Besides, she asked him to bring her here. So we have no right to touch him or do anything to him."

Stepping from the grounded rowboat, Mrs. Dexter looked curiously up and down the wooded shore. Then her eyes traveled inland, taking in the grassy slopes and rugged shrubbery.

"What an ideal camping spot," she cried. "Mother would adore it."

"It'll soon be Mr. Cliffe's summer home," I told her. "For he bought it for that purpose."

"Jerry," she smiled at me, when I further explained to her that I was a personal friend of the millionaire's, "I sometimes wonder if you fully realize what a lucky boy you are."

"I'm lucky, all right," I smiled at her in return, "to have friends like you and your

mother. For she bakes the swellest fried cakes
I ever tasted.''

"And has it never occurred to you," she
added, "that the reason *why* we have such a
warm interest in you is because we know that
you're a good boy?''

Which was pretty nice of her, I thought. And
to show my appreciation I relieved her of the
black leather bag that she carried, taking it
over to one of the newly erected pup tents,
which, I explained, was the only shelter available, unless she preferred to sleep in a cave.

"Oh," she enthused, "I adore sleeping under
canvas. I always did. Is it your tent, Jerry?''
she showed added interest.

"Yes, ma'am," I nodded, putting the bag inside on the ground. Then I showed her how
to fix the netting so that the mosquitoes
coudn't get at her.

"But where will *you* sleep?'' she further inquired.

"With Red.''

"And you're sure," she pinned me down,
"that you won't be over-crowded?''

"If we are," I grinned, "I'll kick him out.''

Bid had just as big an opinion of himself
as ever. We never could have pulled the "po-
tato-peeling'' trick on *him,* he blustered. Nor
could we have stuffed *him* with the ghost story.

Which prompted Mrs. Dexter to inquire, with a curious look at us, if we really had seen a ghost.

"Chet Milden did," Scoop spoke up, unwilling, of course, to tell the truth about the "ghost" in front of the enemy chief.

"Bunk!" the latter grunted contemptuously.

"You don't believe in ghosts, huh?"

"No, nor in fairies, either."

"How about Santa Claus?" grinned Scoop.

"Is that supposed to be funny?"

"Sure thing," Red put in. "Haw, haw, haw!"

"Where is it?" Bid looked around.

"What?"

"The mirror."

"What mirror?"

"I thought you saw yourself in the mirror."

"*Me?*" Red then caught on. "Say," he colored up, "I'll sock you one, if you throw any more slams at me."

Al tackled Bid about the stolen plate.

"Where is it?" he demanded, looking out for himself.

"Where's what?"

"Our plate."

"*Your* plate," the boatman sneered. "Let me tell one."

"Yes, *our* plate," Al shoved out his jaw, to

show the enemy that he meant business. "What have you done with it?"

Mrs. Dexter then spoke up, on our side, telling us that she had the plate in her leather bag. And furious over the way things were working against him, Bid grabbed the oars, with a final hateful look at us, and started off.

But he soon experienced difficulties. And I wondered at this. His eyes, as he pulled savagely on the oars, stood out like halved onions. But the harder he worked the less progress he made.

"Why don't you come back and start over again?" suggested Peg.

"Aw, shut up."

"Bid, that's the easiest thing you can say."

"SHUT UP, I tell you."

"What seems to be the trouble?"

"None of your business."

"Boy, you sure are working."

"I'll tell the world," Red chimed in.

"Look at him sweat, fellows."

"His tongue will be hanging out next."

"Like a dog, huh?"

"Sure thing."

And so we kept it up. For it was fun for us. But Bid wasn't wholly dumb. And looking around, suspicious of a trick, he found that he was dragging an old concrete anchor that

Peg had cleverly hooked on the back of the boat.

"You needn't bother to bring it back," purred old hefty, as the furious boatman unfastened the weight. "Just drop it in the canal, dearie. When we want it Red will dive for it."

"I'd like to sock you with it."

"Yah, I dare say you would. But don't try throwing it from there. For it's pretty hefty for a little guy like you. And you might accidentally lose your balance and fall in. Not that we care particularly about *you*. But we'd hate to have you fall on some poor little froggy and bend him out of shape."

"You think you're smart."

"Well, maybe we are. Anyway, we established a good record this afternoon as rotten-egg shooters."

"Haw, haw, haw!" Red applauded.

"Let me tell you something," Bid fumed. "We're still here—the whole gang of us. And we're going to stay here, too."

"How lovely."

"Furthermore, we're going to clean up on you guys, if it takes us six months."

"You'll need to do some 'cleaning,' all right, like your chums did this afternoon, if you get within range of our rotten-egg shooter."

"Your name will be mud when we get through with you."

"Spelt with a capital 'M,' huh?"

"You'll find out."

"Well, Bid, we can stand as much as you can. But don't squeal, kid, if you get the worst of it."

"You never made me squeal yet."

"No? How about last night at the spring when I socked you on the beezer?"

"You missed me by a mile."

"Oh, I did, did I?"

"You heard me say so."

Al turned to Mrs. Dexter.

"Did you pay him any money for the plate?"

"No. Until I knew for sure that it belonged to the long-lost set, which seems probable, but which has yet to be proved, I was unwilling to set a price on it."

Asked then by the eager collector if we had lifted the balance of the treasure, we waited a moment or two until Bid was out of hearing and then told her the truth about the empty spring. The silver, we said, had been lifted that afternoon by the "ghost," who then had mysteriously sealed himself in a cave.

"How amazing," she cried, with startled eyes.

"Jerry thinks the hunchback is a voodooer," the leader further informed.

"A voodooer?" she searched our faces. "What do you mean?"

I told her about Mrs. Morrison.

"Your mother knew her well. She was with her when she died."

"Oh, yes! I remember now. Mrs. Morrison was the old lady who owned this island."

"Hers was a queer religion," I added. "Like witchcraft. That's how she was able to predict her own death."

"And she really did that?"

"Your mother says she did."

"I was living in Chicago when Mrs. Morrison died. Mother probably wrote and told me about the funeral and the queer things that preceded it. But if she did I had forgotten all about it."

"Then you didn't know Mrs. Morrison yourself?"

"I met her once or twice during my visits to Tutter. But I have no clear recollection of her."

"And you have no idea who the hunchback is?"

"No."

"Didn't she have a husband?"

"Of course. But he died many years ago."

"And you never heard that he had a crooked back?"

"No."

"Evidently," laughed Scoop, following my questions, "Jerry's beginning to think that the hunchback is a real ghost."

There was more scattered talk about "voodooism" and *"netiks."* Then, while our visitor dabbled around the fire with a frying pan and coffee pot, getting herself a late supper, we fixed up a comfortable grass bed for her, after which, with other and more important work ahead of us, it being our daring scheme to explore the sealed cave, we rowed to the west marsh in the fading daylight where we gathered an armful of cat-tails. Later these natural "torches" were partially dried over the fire and then soaked in melted grease, that being the only substitute we had for kerosene.

Still, the grease torches, so far as I could see, were almost as good as others we had made, for other work, dipped in kerosene. And taking my two I then crossed the island to the north shore and got into the skiff. For having drawn the long straw, at the last moment, it was my job to work alone. I didn't like it. I wanted to be one of the explorers. But a fellow doesn't always get the job that he wants.

"All set, Jerry?" the leader inquired, as I got ready to shove off.

"Yes."

"Got your torches?"

"Yes."

"And plenty of matches?"

"Yes."

"You have two hours of darkness before the moon comes up. So you ought to be able to creep into the Strickers' camp without them seeing you. Listen carefully. Find out all you can about their plans. We'll signal to you when our work is done. But if they start for the island before we signal, run down the shore and light one of your own torches. Red will be watching. And as soon as he gets your signal he'll scoot for the cave to warn us of the coming attack."

I nodded.

"Let's shake, Jerry," he then suggested.

I held out my hand.

"Scoop," I shivered, thinking of the sealed cave, which in the darkness would be a thousand times more mysterious than ever, "this is blamed risky stuff."

"I know it."

"I wish I was going to be with you."

"I'll have Peg and Al."

"But you may need me, too."

"Your work is important, Jerry. And, in a way, it's just as risky as ours."

"What'll you do," I further shivered, "if the hunchback tackles you?"

"Fight him, of course."

"But he may have a gun."

There was a moment's deep silence. Then a carp flopped in the darkness, sending a cold chill down my backbone.

"Well, so-long, Jerry. Do your best. We're depending on you."

"So-long, Scoop."

I again took his hand. And I squeezed it tight. Then, the darkness favoring my purpose, I gritted my teeth and set out.

CHAPTER XVI

THE MAN IN THE WHITE BOAT

DIPPING my oars in even muffled strokes I silently crossed the darkened wide waters to the north shore. It didn't take me many minutes. For it wasn't far. And then, sort of hugging the dim wooded bank, I worked west and south.

The shore at this point was like the inside of a hoop—sort of circular-like. Little knobs of land stuck out here and there, more or less wooded like the rest of the adjacent country, and in places there were little bays, some of which, I imagine, were creeks, the smaller ends of which had crawled far into the spreading forest. I had to go around the knobs. But I didn't bend into the bays. I just steered a straight course across them at the mouth, picking up the darkened shore on the opposite side.

Camping is more fun when a fellow can discover things. And so a trip of this kind would have been bully good sport in the daytime. Or, under ordinary circumstances, with some one for company, I would have enjoyed the trip at night. For we frequently prowl around that way in the dark, in secret exploration, espe-

cially when the bullheads are biting. But to-
night, as I have said, I was peculiarly fidgety.

Once I rammed into a log. And my first
crazy thought was that I had struck a floating
corpse. Gee-miny crickets! This was no
time to think of corpses. I started counting
sheep. One, two, three, four, five, six. And
suddenly the sheep turned into ghosts. Ghosts,
mind you, jumping over a stone wall. Of all
the crazy junk!

To add to my mental hilarity, as you might
say, the neighborhood bats got their tricky
eyes on me. And though I couldn't see them
in the darkness, as they very plainly saw me,
I could hear them zipping over my head. Were
they trying to see how close they could come to
me without socking me? Or was it their jolly
little game to keep coming closer and closer
until they finally walloped me?

Oof! A bat is a filthy thing. Almost as bad
as a rat. And how awful it would be, I thought,
with a squeamish shiver, to have one of them
mush me in the face. Bats and corpses! Beautiful thoughts, surely. It was a pity I couldn't
think of something good to eat, like Red.

Then I ducked to save my life. For something big and black zipped over my head. Like
a young house. *Oh!* . . . I started breathing,
again. For it was only an owl. Still, I didn't

like the way it clicked its bill. What it could do to a fellow's ears, huh? . . . I wisely pulled down my cap.

A pair of glassy green eyes showed up ahead of me on the bank and then melted into the forest. I saw moving shapes, too. And long, wriggly things swam nimbly out of my way as the skiff sliced a path in the inky water. Night time is breakfast, dinner and supper time in animal land. But thank goodness there was nothing here big enough to make a hasty meal of *me*.

I thought of my chums on the island, Red standing guard on the south shore, ready, like Paul Revere, to ride and spread the alarm— only, of course, instead of riding he'd run to beat the cars—and the others hacking daringly at the new wall. What would happen to them when they finally penetrated the sealed cavern? Would the hunchback be laying for them in the black passageways? Would he pop them off, one by one? Or, if he had no gun, would he fight them off like a cornered animal?

Truly this had been an exciting trip. One thing after another had jumped at us to draw our attention from our original plans. Instead of quietly settling down in a cave, like Robinson Crusoe, with a dog on one side of our table and a cat on the other, we had forgotten almost that we ever owned a dog or a cat. Where were they? Certainly, we had seen nothing of them since turning them loose on the island. Maybe they had chewed each other up like the famous calico dog and gingham cat. And where was the parrot that we were going to train to say "Robinson Crusoe, poor Robinson Crusoe," and sit on our shoulders while we ate? Where, too, were our vineyards and gourd plantations and maize fields?

Still, I wasn't sorry that we had met Al, however much our acquaintance with him had upset our original plans. Good kid that he was, he deserved our help. And my big hope was that we'd be able to save the treasure for him, after which, if Scoop and Peg were saved from the hospital, we possibly could settle down to more peaceful adventures.

The light of the enemy's camp fire spread out over the water. And wanting to take no chances that might lead to my detection I presently pulled to shore, securing my skiff under a leaning tree, the washed roots of which, as I climbed over them, made me think of petrified snakes. Then having thus landed, and marking the spot in my mind so that I would have no trouble finding it again, even if I came back on the fly, I gripped my torches and started down the uneven shore.

At places I found myself in marsh hay almost as high as my head. Nor did I enjoy slipping around among the bogs. But there wasn't a great deal of this. For the most part I had firm hard footing. The bushes, too, provided plenty of shelter. So I was safe.

Jimmy was tending the fire. I could see him through the shrubbery, though, as you can imagine, I was very careful not to let him spot me. Heads stuck up here and there, showing where the others were lolling around the fire, as boys do in camp. Still, I could count only five. And that kind of worried me, the more so when I learned that the missing one was Jum Prater. For he's their best spy. But my anxiety soon melted away. For there was mention of a well. And I learned from the further conversation that Jum, after spilling the drinking water, had been sent off in one of the rowboats with the empty pail.

Noticeably uneasy, Bid got up and went down to the shore where, for several minutes, he stood looking across at the camp fire on the island.

"See anything of them?" Jimmy inquired, when the leader came back to the fire.

"No," Bid grunted shortly.

"I bet they're watching us."

"Probably. And that's why I say we'll get

the worst of it if we try sneaking up on them in the dark. For they'll spot us that quick," the speaker snapped his fingers, "if we stick together. And if we separate we're doomed."

"But we've *got* to do something," cried Jimmy. "We can't sit here like ninnies and let them get away with everything."

"If you were so blamed anxious to do something," scowled Bid, "why didn't you do it this morning when you had the chance?"

In the further talk mention was made of our new chum.

"Did I tell you, Bid," Jimmy addressed his cousin, "that we got a line on the new kid this morning?"

"Well, what of it?"

"His name is Alfred Moore. And the others talked as though the treasure belonged to him. So he must be a relative of the old innkeeper's."

"The treasure would be ours," Bid clung to his grievance, "if you fellows had done as I said. Instead, though, you acted like a lot of simpletons. As though the spring really was haunted! Gosh! The more I think of the way you messed up this deal the madder I get."

"Well, get mad and stay mad if you want to," Jimmy spoke independently. "What you say doesn't hurt anybody. As for running from ghosts, I haven't forgotten the time that Jerry Todd chased you down the Oak Island hill.''

No, nor had the "ghost," himself, as he lay there in the weeds with sharpened ears, forgotten about that clever trick. Boy, we sure had fun that night. Bid ran so fast to escape the old hermit's ghost that he lost his own shadow.

Here a white rowboat came quietly into sight. I thought at first that it was Jum. Yet I was puzzled by the rower's guarded movements. He seemed peculiarly anxious to make not the slightest sound.

Then my heart gave a bound. It wasn't Jum at all. It was a man. And he was sitting in the boat listening. That is why he was keeping so quiet.

It couldn't be the hunchback. For he was in the cave. Besides, from what little I could see of the man, as he carefully kept his boat on the fringe of the puddle of light, he seemed not to be deformed.

"What of it?" Bid blustered, when the others further razzed him about running down hill.

"Yes, *what of it?*" Jimmy got up on his ear. "When *you* get scared of a ghost it's all right. But when *we* get scared it's all wrong.''

"But you should have known that the ghost was a trick.''

"It wasn't a trick. Chet actually saw it."

"I'll tell the world," a head was lifted into sight. "It acted just like a real ghost—sort of creepy-like. And then it vanished."

"Into thin air, I suppose," sneered Bid.

"Sure thing," Chet lied cheerfully.

"Oh, you guys give me a pain," Hib Milden spoke up. "Why don't you quit chewing the rag and talk sense?"

"*Him?*" Bid further sneered at Chet. "How can he talk sense when he hasn't got any sense?"

"He's my brother," Hib stiffened.

"Well," Bid's eyes were steady, "what do you mean by that?"

"If you pick on him you pick on me, too."

"Oh! . . . Between the two of you, you think you can lick me, huh?"

"Listen here, Bid," Hib spoke in good sense. "We'll never gain anything by fighting. We've got to stick together. So quit razzing Chet. Maybe he *did* pull a boner. Maybe we all did, for that matter. But it's done. And it can't be undone."

"I was a dumb-bell," Bid admitted, "to go off and leave you. Still, it was necessary. Certainly, I never dreamed for one instant but what the prisoners would be safe in your hands until I got back."

"How would it be," Jimmy then suggested, "if we attacked them just before daybreak? They'll be the sleepiest then."

"I'm just wondering," Bid reflected, "if they aren't liable to lift the treasure to-night and rush it into Steam Corners. For they'd never dare to pass here with it. And if they once got their hands on it they'd be afraid to keep it on the island."

"Then you think we ought to secretly move our camp to the east shore?"

"Not necessarily. But it wouldn't do any harm to spend the night there. And to fool them into thinking that we're all here we can build up a big fire. Or, better still, we can leave some one here to keep the fire going."

"Hot-dog!" cried Jimmy. "I have the feeling that we're going to win out yet. And if we do win out, and get our hands on the treasure, we're going to dig for home and dig *quick*."

"But how about that Moore kid?" one of the gang spoke up. "If he's a relative of the old innkeeper's, as you say, doesn't that give him first claim on the silver?"

"The fellow who has first claim on it," Bid gave his opinion, "is the fellow who gets it."

"Then if we get it, it's ours, huh?"

"Absolutely."

There was more talk about the treasure. And

watching the mysterious boatman, with fast-beating heart and puzzled wits, I fancied at times that his hands trembled greedily as they gripped the motionless oars.

Then, with a single silent stroke, he shot away into the darkness, his keen ears having detected other oarlocks.

It was Jum this time.

"Say," the newcomer panted, slopping water all the way from the boat to the fire, "did you guys see anything of an old geezer in a white boat?"

"No."

"I ran into him in the canal. And what do you know if he didn't grab me by the neck and start choking. I let out a squawk. Then, when he got a squint at me with his flashlight, he let me go. He was looking for another kid, he said, who had stolen his horse. I think it's that new kid on the island. For he called me by the other's name in the dark."

Gee-miny crickets! I knew now who the mysterious boatman was. And I knew, too, why he had stretched his ears so greedily at every mention of our chum's fortune.

It was old Clud, the grasping slave driver from Indiana.

CHAPTER XVII

AROUND THE CAMP FIRE

AL's young strength was a gold mine to the grasping Indiana farmer, which explains why the man had come all this distance to head off the runaway and forcibly drag him back to farm slavery. Then, too, dogged, relentless skunk that he was, a miser at heart and entirely lacking in the pity that most men have for an orphan boy, he itched to overtake the defenseless runaway to soundly punish him for his flight.

I was fighting mad now. A fellow gets that way when a bully starts shoving his chum around. And, to that point, if Clud wasn't a bully I'd like to have you show me one. The miserable old whelp! Fortune had favored him in his search for the runaway. But let him try mistreating our new chum if he dared and see what he'd get. Gr-r-r-r! It would be lovely, I thought, to tickle the top of his bean with a nice fat club. Or, if he tried any funny business with our treasure, he'd get something even worse than a clubbing.

What I better do, I sensibly decided, instead

of staying here, was to get back to the island
as quickly as I knew how. First I'd warn Al
of his danger. Then, if my chums were trapped
in the cave, as was not improbable, we'd pitch
in and rescue them. Or, if they had successfully recovered the treasure (and what a
happy thought that was!), we'd flop it out of
sight in a jiffy. After which old skinflint and
the hunchbacked "voodooer" could do their
worst.

The Strickers gave me no concern. For I
knew exactly what to expect from them. And
putting them out of my mind for the present,
in favor of the more pressing job of carrying
the news back to the island, I lit out down the
shore as tight as I could go. Stopping in the
first sheltered bay I lit my torches, thus signaling Red that I was on my way back. He
would take it from this that the enemy was
planning an attack. But that was all right.
We had as much to fear from old doo-funny as
we had from the Zulutown gang.

Getting Red's answering signal I then
jumped into my skiff and grabbed the oars. It
wasn't so dark now. For the moon was getting ready to come up. So I had no trouble
laying a direct course to the island's north
shore, where I intended to land near the spring.

The white boat had entirely disappeared.

And I wondered uneasily if the miser had already landed on the island. What if he surprised the procession of treasure bearers coming out of the cave? Gee! He might get the upper hands of them before they fully realized their peril. Still, having gotten my signal, they'd be on their guard.

To my great joy Scoop and Peg were waiting for me near the spring. And jumping from the skiff, the moment it grounded on the gravelly beach, I asked them excitedly where Al was.

"He and Red are picketing the south shore," Scoop told me.

"Yes," Peg put in quickly, "and *we* better hurry over there, too, if the Strickers are coming."

"It isn't the Strickers," I cried, in continued excitement. "It's old Clud."

Scoop was a moment or two fixing the name in his memory.

"Not the man from Indiana!" he cried, in growing dismay.

"No one else but," I waggled. "And he knows about the treasure, too. For he overheard the Strickers talking about it."

Getting my complete story, the others then told me about their own disappointing work. Penetrating the sealed cave, with thumping hearts, they had found not the slightest trace of the hunchback. Nor had they found any trace of the treasure. Instead of having mysteriously sealed himself in the cave, as we had suspected, the "voodooer," after lifting the silver, had undoubtedly skinned out. Where he was now we had not the slightest idea. But it was our belief he was many miles away.

So, as you can see, he wasn't a "voodooer" after all—just a plain, ordinary crook. Which shows how easy it is for even a Juvenile Jupiter Detective to go wrong in his deductions. Still, the sealed cave was a peculiar thing. We were unable to explain it; also the hunchback's knowledge of the silver's peculiar hiding place. There was mystery surrounding him that probably never would be cleared up.

Al's heart was broken, I was told. Expecting so much in penetrating the cave, he now had nothing. Nor had he anything much to look forward to. For there was little chance of the hunchback being captured.

"But maybe there's some secret part of the cave that you haven't explored?" I hung on hopefully.

Scoop shook his head.

"No, Jerry. We searched the cavern from beginning to end. It's entirely empty, both of the hunchback and the treasure."

"But how did he get away?" my bewilderment deepened.

"He must have had a hidden boat."

Like the others I felt pretty blue when we crossed the island to tell Al the added bad news. Poor kid! We sure had a big hunk of affection for him, as I have mentioned. And it made me sick to think that we were unable to help him, which doesn't mean, though, that we had any intention of surrendering him to old Clud. I guess not! The more I thought about that unprincipled old horned toad the more I itched to land on his hat rack with a sizable baseball bat.

"If Al is big enough to work on a farm," I told the others, as we hurried along the moonlit path to the south bay, whose silvered surface showed here and there through the drooping trees, "he's big enough to work in a brick factory. And Dad will gladly give him a job when he hears our story."

"Or he can get a job in our store," was Scoop's counter suggestion.

"Maybe that would be better," I considered, thinking of the long workday that the brickmakers put in. "For then he could go to school."

"He's a swell kid," Peg spoke up. "I wish he'd come and live with me. We'd have fun wearing each other's clothes. And I have a big bed all to myself.''

Once before we had picked up a kid who was down and out. That was Poppy Ott. To-day old Poppy is one of the brightest and best-liked boys in Tutter. All he needed was a chance to show what he could do. So, as you can see, it pays to help other boys less fortunate than yourself. Even more than that, it's a sort of duty.

Al turned white when we told him that old Clud was in the wide waters. And I never saw such dumb misery in a fellow's eyes in all my life. I guess he was trying to fight down the feeling that God had completely forsaken him. When a fellow loses *that* hope, let me tell you, he sure is a goner.

Strangely, though, nothing was seen of the white rowboat. Where had Clud disappeared to? Having landed secretly on the island, was he now lurking in the bushes to grab Al on the sly? Or, more important in his grasping mind, was he waiting to see where we had the treasure put away? Well, was my thought, he was fooled there. For we had no treasure except the one silver plate. . . . I was glad he didn't know about that.

Later we saw the Strickers' two rowboats steal away from their camp and sort of detour to the east shore, where they probably lay in hiding throughout the night, hoping, of course, that we would attempt to pass them with the recovered treasure. The silly boobs! Bid had talked big about what he and his gang were going to do to us. But it was plainly to be seen that they were afraid of us. Still, they might get up sufficient courage later on to plan an attack, secret or otherwise. But we should worry. Given any kind of a chance at all we could lick the stuffing out of them. Besides, we would be on our guard.

Mrs. Dexter had kept the camp fire going, finding a keen joy, I imagine, in her rugged surroundings. And now, in joining her beside the roaring fire, we found that she had made a sort of taffy candy from our supply of molasses and sugar. Ordered to wash our hands, we then helped her pull the taffy until it was firm and white (only ours didn't get quite as white as hers), after which we had the jolly good fun of eating it.

It was a big disappointment to her, of course, that the King's Silver had been spirited away from the island by the hunchback. But she had the good sense not to keep talking about it in front of Al. For she realized that his disappointment over the loss of the treasure was a thousand times more bitter than hers. Like us,

she felt sorry for him. And when she offered
to buy the single plate for twelve hundred dollars, I suspected that she was paying more than
it was worth. But that was all right. Rich as
she was, she could find no better way of spending her money.

So Al was worth twelve hundred dollars. A
mere drop in the bucket, as you might say, to
what he had expected. Still, twelve hundred
dollars is twelve hundred dollars. Not many
boys have that much jack. The money was to
be deposited to his credit in one of the Tutter
banks, to be drawn out as he needed it. And
in further kindness the rich woman insisted on
taking the orphan boy into her own home.

"I'm not a lawyer," she told him, as he sat
beside her in front of the cheerful fire, "but I
doubt very much if this farmer from whom you
ran away, claiming mistreatment, has any legal
right to force you to return with him if you
prefer otherwise, and can prove to the local
authorities that you are self-supporting. For
it doesn't seem constitutional to me that the
laws of any state would condone any such unfair persecution of a minor as that. However,
as I say, I am not technically informed. And
it may be that the papers you mention, signed
by Mr. Clud when he took you out of the poorhouse, are more binding than I realize. If he

is your legal guardian the law, I suppose, will expect you to obey him as long as he, himself, is fair and trustworthy. Which would mean, in case he further mistreated you, that the law would give you prompt redress.''

"But how can the law help me," Al spoke bitterly, "if he kills and robs me?"

"What we better do, I think," Scoop spoke up, in good leadership, "is to hit for Tutter to-morrow morning in the old scow. That will fool the Strickers, who, of course, will think that we have the treasure aboard. And with six of us against him, including Mrs. Dexter, old Clud had better keep a safe distance from us."

"Yes," smiled our visitor, "don't overlook me. For I can swing a wicked club, if necessary."

"Evidently the burglars around Tutter know that," I spoke to a particular point.

"And you were so sure, Jerry," she quickly caught my meaning, "that I was going to be robbed."

"It isn't too late yet," I told her.

"I'd hate to be the burglar," she further smiled, "who attempted to intrude on Mother. For she's a champion shot with boiling water."

"It's a pity," grunted Scoop, from his place

WHAT IF HE SURPRISED THE TREASURE BEARERS COMING
OUT OF THE CAVE?

Jerry Todd Pirate.

Page 201

beside the fire, "that she couldn't use some of her boiling water on old Clud."

As we had suspected, the farmer had secretly landed on the island. Furthermore, he had been listening to us, depending for concealment on the fringing trees and bushes. And now, at mention of his name by our leader, he stepped boldly into sight.

First to catch sight of him, Mrs. Dexter screamed at the top of her voice. Gosh! That alone, considering how worked-up we were, was enough to scare the wits out of us. As for Al, I never saw a whiter kid in all my life.

But instead of batting the runaway over the head, the shuffling old man was as nice as pie.

"Howdy, Alfy?" he held out a hairy hand which matched the shaggy eyebrows. "Awful glad to see you ag'in, Alfy," the name was repeated with a peculiar drawl. "Me an' Ma has bin awful lonesome since you left. We jest couldn't content ourselves nohow. There was your empty chair at the table, a constant reminder of our loss. An' there was your empty hook behind the kitchen door where you always kept your cap. So, unable to stand it any longer, I finally set out to look fur you, rememberin' that your ma's people come from here, which I figured was a natural-enough place fur you to head to. An' here I be, happy, as I say, to find you safe an' sound."

This slick talk didn't fool any of the open-mouthed listeners, least of all Al, himself. For the sort of exultant look in the half-hidden green eyes didn't match the honeyed words at all. Scoop, though, as quick with his wits as ever, let on that he was fooled.

"Why! . . ." the clever leader gave a glad cry. "If here isn't Mr. Clud. Can you imagine anything more *wonderful?* We were just talking about you, Mr. Club—I mean Mr. Clud. Al has been *so* homesick to see you. Haven't you, *Alfy* dear?"

But "Alfy dear" was struck dumb, which he probably wouldn't have been if he had known Scoop as well as we did.

"See?" further beamed the young actor. "He's so choked up with emotion over your unexpected appearance that he can't say a word. But his joyful eyes speak for themselves. And how is dear Mrs. Clud?—Mamma Clud, as Alfy so affectionately calls her. We've heard such *wonderful* things about her. Nothing that we can cook for Al—I mean Alfy—is half as good as the delicious meals that he got at your house. Apple dumplings smothered in yellow cream, strawberry shortcake, ice cream three times a week, and *every* morning a heap-

ing plate of Aunt Jemima's wonderful pancakes, soaking in country butter and Vermont
maple syrup. He has told us all about it, even
to the mustard pickles."

At first apparently struck dumb like poor
Al, the farmer now pushed out a noticeable
scowl.

"Um . . ." he muttered, showing a sudden
dislike for the glib speaker. "Alfy mayn't 'a'
got a big variety of fancy trimmings at our
table, but he always got plenty of good sub-
stantial food. In that, as in everything else,
we always tried to do what was best fur him.
An' while I may have lost my temper now an'
then, an' talked cross to him, they hain't
a-goin' to be no more of that. We want him
to come home because we love him like our
own son."

This brought Al back to earth.

"Yes," he cried, with flashing eyes, "you
love me a lot, *you* do."

"Now, Alfy," drawled Scoop, slyly kicking
the other in the shins, "that's no way for you
to talk to Papa, after him coming all this distance to make up with you. Of course, he loves
you. And he loves your twelve hundred dollars, too—don't you, Mr. Dub?—I mean Mr.
Club—no," Scoop tried frantically to get the
right name, "I mean Mr. Clud."

"Heh?" the old man stared, though not without a crafty look in his eyes. "Twelve hundred dollars, you say? What twelve hundred dollars be you talkin' about?"

As though he didn't already know about the twelve hundred dollars!—with those sharp ears of his.

"Haven't you heard about Alfy's fortune, Mr. Club?—I mean Mr. Clud. His grandmother buried a lot of valuable silver dishes in a spring. A hunchback got away with everything except one plate, which this lady has just bought for twelve hundred dollars. And the money is all yours, isn't it, Alfy dear?"

Al knew that our smart leader wasn't kicking him for nothing.

"Yes," he nodded, hoping for the best.

"Um . . ." the miser rubbed his hands. "Twelve hundred dollars, you say. I'm glad to hear this, Alfy. An' has the nice lady paid you yet?"

"No," Mrs. Dexter spoke up, as trustful of Scoop as we were. "It has been agreed that I'm to deposit the money in a Tutter bank."

"Um . . . Alfy will want me to take charge of the money fur him. I kin put it out at interest an' make it earn more money fur him."

Scoop rolled his eyes sorrowfully.

"We sure will miss little Alfy when he's

good spanking. The very idea! How do you suppose *he* feels, nice old gentleman that he is, to have you act this way? You ought to be ashamed of yourself.''

"Aw! . . ." the scolded one further rebelled, unwilling to place too much confidence in the leader's unknown scheme.

"Go on," hissed Scoop. "He won't dare to harm you, if that's what's eating you. And when he's asleep slit a hole in the back of the tent and crawl out.''

CHAPTER XVIII

TREASURE ISLAND!

WE finally got Al to bed in the ogre's tent, and then, after a few hurried words with Mrs. Dexter, Scoop and I and Red crawled into the remaining small tent where for more than an hour we lay in complete silence except for an occasional guarded whisper.

Then, about eleven-thirty, Peg tiptoed into the supposedly sleeping camp.

"I found the white rowboat," he told us, wedging into the crowded tent. "It was tied to a bush in the marsh."

"Did you move it?" the leader inquired, thinking of the important use to which the rowboat was going to be put later on.

"Sure thing. It's down on the beach this minute."

"If you're so good at moving things," squirmed Red, "why don't you let up on my face for a chance and move your elbows some place else?"

Peg pretended astonishment.

"*What?* Are you here?" Then he further draped himself on the helpless one. "I thought your head was a red sofa pillow,'' he added complacently.

"Big boy, you'd suffer for this if I had a stout pin.''

"How does it come you aren't eating?''

"Gee!'' the tone was noticeably brighter. "I never thought of that. . . . Did you eat that extra piece of cherry pie, Jerry?''

"*Good* night!'' Scoop tore his hair. "If you aren't the limit. Here we are with the job on our hands of saving Al's life. And all *you* can think of is *cherry pie.*''

Which reminded the hungry one of an old tune.

"Can you make a cherry pie, Billy boy, Billy boy; can you make a cherry pie, Billy boy? Yes, I can make a cherry pie, quick as a cat can wink its eye; I can make a cherry pie, Billy boy.''

"One more 'Billy boy' out of you,'' threatened Scoop, with murder in his eyes, "and I'll choke you till your Adam's apple pushes the top of your head off.''

"Where's Al?'' inquired Peg. "Why doesn't he hurry up?''

"He's waiting for old poodle-face to go to sleep.''

"Maybe he is asleep. Let's take a look.''

"*Lay down,* you big nut, and keep still.''

Then the other voice piped up again.

"Did I ever tell you about the swell cherry pie I ate at——"

"Oh, Red, you aren't funny."

"Tell it to us to-morrow at dinner," grinned Peg, mussing up the freckled one's fiery hair, "and we'll pretend it's dessert."

"Listen, fellows, this is no time for nonsense."

"Of course not," Red agreed promptly.

"Well, then, keep still."

"You're doing the most of the talking."

"Oh, *shut up.*"

"It was a lucky thing for us that Bid and his gang took it into their heads to cross the lake," I then spoke up, following Peg's report that the enemy's two rowboats were still parked on the east shore. "Otherwise Al might have had some trouble passing their camp."

"He would have been safe enough, I think, with Mrs. Dexter in the boat."

"Is she going, too?" Peg inquired of the leader.

"Sure thing."

"But what will old fuss-budget say to-morrow morning when he learns that they skinned out in his boat?"

"We should worry what *he* says."

"We're liable to lose our own boat."

"Well, what of it? It's nothing but an old tub. That's why I suggested that we hunt up the other one. For the quicker Al and Mrs. Dexter get back to Tutter the better for them."

Here we caught the sound of ripping cloth.

"It's Al!" breathed Scoop, stretching his ears.

Following a short deep silence, in which we scarcely breathed for fear our plans might miscarry at the last moment, we heard the sound again. Then, after another and longer silence, a shadow crossed the door of our tent.

"Hi," a grinning face peeked in at us.

"How's Papa?" Scoop grinned in return, showing in the tone of his voice how great was his relief over the other's successful escape.

"Dead to the world."

"We heard you cut the tent."

"Yes, and I was scared stiff that *he, too,* would hear me. But luckily for me he never stirred."

Mrs. Dexter knew about our plans. For, as I have mentioned, we had talked with her. And now, alive to what was going on in the camp, she quietly joined us on the beach,

cheerfully willing, like the brave good woman
that she was, to do everything in her power to
help us save our orphaned chum from the
ogre's clutches.

"Don't forget to call up Dad when you get
home," I told her, as I dropped the black
leather bag at her feet in the back of the rowboat. "He'll be glad to help you. For he
knows Al. You can rely on Mr. Ellery, too."

"Have no doubt, Jerry, that everything will
be done to safeguard your chum that can be
done."

"And you're *sure*," I pinned her down,
"that you won't let Clud take him away
from you?"

"Yes," she spoke with peculiar grimness,
"I am *very* sure of that."

I then leaned over and whispered to her.

"Mrs. Dexter," I said, looking into her eyes,
"you're bully. And any time you want your
grass cut or your windows washed just flash
the word to me and I'll be Johnny-on-the-
spot. It won't cost you a cent, either."

"Jerry," she intended that I should see how
well she liked me, "you're one of the dearest
boys I've ever known."

"Well, I don't know how *dear* I am," I
grinned, "but I sure know how to twist the
tail of a lawn mower."

"Do you know why I have taken such a fancy to Al?" she then inquired, with a whimsical expression.

"Why?" I curiously inquired in turn.

"Because he's so much like you."

"His feet are bigger," I grinned.

"Possibly. But I doubt if his heart is. For I don't know how it could be."

"I'll be over to see you as soon as I get home."

"Al and I will be looking for you."

This reference to our chum aroused more reflective thoughts.

"You really need a boy in your home, Mrs. Dexter," I told her, with an earnest nod.

"Yes," she smiled in a way that made me think that an added happiness had come into her life, "I'm beginning to think so myself."

Al was ready to step into the boat and start off.

"Well, good-by, old hunk," I shoved out my mitt. "We'll see you later on."

Quickly grasping the extended hand he squeezed it until it hurt. But that was all right. I liked it, though if Bid Stricker had pinched me half as hard I would have knocked his block off.

"Gee, Jerry," he loved me with his eyes, "you're a swell pal. I'll never forget this.

And when I get my money I'm going to divvy up with you, too."

Imagine *him* saying that, poor kid that he was! But, of course, *he* would. For he was that kind of a boy. However, though I had a few set ideas on the subject myself I didn't argue with him. We could do that later on.

There was more warm hand shaking, after which Al seated himself for the long row. I gave him a shove, calling a final good-by to him. And then, as the fast-moving rowboat grew smaller and smaller on the moonlit lake, finally disappearing from our sight into the westward canal, I turned away with a peculiar emptiness inside of me where my heart was.

"Sleepy?" Scoop inquired, as we walked back to camp.

"Yes," I nodded.

"Al's a good kid, Jerry," he matched my own thoughts.

"You're blamed tootin'."

"I bet we miss him."

"I miss him already," I said simply.

We might have saved ourselves the sleepy job of standing guard by turns throughout the balance of the night. For the Strickers made no attempt to attack us. At daybreak we saw them dejectedly crossing the wide waters to their camp. And later, to our great surprise, they completely packed up and pulled out for home.

Waking up at seven-thirty, while we were enjoying our breakfast, old Clud stretched himself in the warm morning sunshine as it poured into his open tent. The pleasant day with its summery drone and lively bird chorus matched his spirits. Soon now he and the helpless orphan would be on their way home with the twelve hundred dollars. Um. . . . Twelve hundred dollars! He hadn't expected any such good fortune as this in his search for the runaway. And how disappointing that the rest of the valuable silver had been stolen. Still, twelve hundred dollars was a lot of money. He was very well satisfied. Um. . . . A little hand rubbing, and so on.

Such, I imagine, was the substance of his drowsy thoughts. Then, in wider awakening, he made discoveries in the tent that convinced him that the day wasn't as sunny and bright as he had let himself believe. For the slit in the tent's canvas back told its own story of the midnight escape of the supposedly trapped slave and his coveted bank roll.

"A conspiracy!" the tricked one thundered, descending on us with fiery eyes. "A dirty, low-down conspiracy."

"No," corrected Scoop, sinking his teeth

into the edge of one of Peg's choice leatherette pancakes, "it isn't a conspiracy—it's breakfast. Would you like some cornflakes and condensed milk, Mr. Club?—I mean Mr. Clud. Or would you prefer milkflakes and condensed corn?"

"Where is he?" the voice further thundered. "An' when did this happen?"

"Goodness gracious!" Scoop arched his eyebrows. "How peevish you are this morning. Didn't you sleep well last night?"

"Where is he, I say?"

"Who?"

"That boy of mine."

"Oh! . . . You mean little *Alfy*."

"Yes," the word was snapped out. "Where is he?"

"On his way to Tutter with Mrs. Dexter."

"An' *you* helped him escape, I s'pose!" the older one's hatred was concentrated.

"Sure thing," Scoop admitted cheerfully.

"Fur two cents," the man showed added rage, "I'd wring your confounded neck, meddlesome gab-box that you are."

"I suppose you thought we'd stand aside like dummies and let you rob Al and everything else, huh? Well, if that's your idea of boys you've got a lot to learn. In this neighborhood we stick up for our chums. And when

they're in trouble we fight for them, too. Put
that in your pipe and smoke it, you old money
grabber.''

The green eyes spit poison.

"If you was my boy I'd break your neck.''

"How lovely for me then that I'm not
your boy.''

"You're goin' to pay dearly fur this before
I git through with you, dratted fools that you
are, the hul parcel of you. What was it your
business, anyway?''

"It was our business because Al is our
chum, as I just told you.''

"The ongrateful young whelp. I'll trim his
hide when I ketch him. You think I kain't
make him go home with me. But I'll show
you. An' I'll show that woman, too, who's
stickin' up fur him. There's a law that pro-
tects farmers from hoss thieves. An' it's a
hard-bound law, too. Let him try further escape on me an' I'll show him a thing or two.
He'll either go home with me, or he'll go to
jail.''

Scoop saw that the cowardly man was afraid
to tackle the four of us.

"Yes,'' came the sneer, "and a swell home
it was, to judge from what Al told us about it.
He didn't even get enough to eat.''

"That's a lie,'' came the furious denial.

"You didn't buy him decent clothes, either."

"An' that's another lie."

"But he's going to get plenty to eat and to wear now. For Mrs. Dexter is going to adopt him."

"She kain't," the man screamed. "Fur I've got first claim on him. An' law is law."

He went off then in search of his rowboat. And failing to find it he came back and took our raft, which he later abandoned in the channel, a short distance away, finding that he could make faster progress afoot.

"He'll be lucky," laughed Scoop, while we were poling the raft home, "if the Tutter business men don't give him a coat of tar and feathers."

"That's what he deserves, all right," I put in.

"What puzzles me," reflected Peg, "is how a man with as much land and money as he has can be so blamed mean. For the farmers I know are jolly, good men."

"Misers are all alike," Scoop said shortly, "wherever you find them."

"Bu-lieve me," piped up Red, "I'm never going to be a miser. For what good is money to a fellow if he doesn't spend it for something good to eat?"

That blamed kid! Sometimes I feel like socking him. Yet I have to laugh at him.

Our treasure-hunting adventures having apparently come to an end, and left in undisputed possession of the island, we put in the day laying out vineyards and sugar-cane plantations. We further explored the cave, too, and hunted unsuccessfully for elephants and monkeys, which was all bully good fun. But I missed old Al.

During an afternoon shower we stripped to the bare skin and gave our mistreated old scow a much-needed bath. It was a stinking job. And at times we held our noses as the rotten-egg fumes percolated around us. But we stuck it out. Later, Red having done a neat trick with the engine, we enjoyed a trip round the island. *Our* island, mind you! I tell you we felt proud.

Shortly after supper we heard a voice calling to us from Tavern Beach. And when we ran to the north shore, there, to our surprise, was Al on the other side of the water, waving to us like a young windmill and yelling at the top of his voice for us to come and get him.

I hadn't been without hope that he would join us later on, when the defeated Indiana snake had cleared out for home. But I certainly hadn't expected to see him so soon.

And I wondered, with a touch of uneasiness, if something had happened to Mrs. Dexter. Still, his actions didn't suggest that.

Rather than wait for the heavy scow to be brought around the island I offered to row across in the skiff, which was close by.

"If he's got any candy," Red called after me, "don't make a pig of yourself and eat it all up, especially if it's gumdrops."

Al lost no time getting into the skiff when it touched the shore.

"Surprise party, huh?" he grinned at me, with the happiest pair of eyes that I ever saw in a boy's face.

"I'll tell the world," I grinned back.

"I've got some big news for you, Jerry."

"You look it."

"Can you imagine, old pal, the balance of the silver is on the island after all."

"*What?*" I cried, staring at him.

"Honest. That's what brought me back so soon. In fact, Mrs. Dexter sent me back. For the man who holds the key to the silver's hiding place is coming to the island to-night to dig it up."

"The hunchback?" I inquired excitedly.

"No. He's a hired man on the Cadman farm. I have a letter from Mrs. Dexter telling you all about it."

Scoop later read the amazing letter aloud:

MY DEAR JERRY AND ALL:

Al is bringing you the most *wonderful* news! The balance of the King's Silver hasn't been stolen at all. It's still hidden on the island.

This afternoon I received a call from a burly, swarthy-faced man by the name of Arnold Peters, a hired man on the farm formerly owned by Al's grandmother, but now in the possession of Andrew Cadman. Cadman, it seems, according to Peters' story, had known for many years that the King's Silver was sunken in the big spring on Oak Island. There is an unexplained reason why the peculiar land owner preferred not to disturb the treasure. Subject to walking and talking in his sleep, proof, *I* should say, of a disturbed or even remorseful mind, he thus unwittingly disclosed the spring's secret. Peters investigated. And finding the silver in the spring he promptly removed it to another hiding place, evidently overlooking the one plate that you boys found.

I craftily questioned him about the treasure's new hiding place, hoping to pick up some important information for you. But he was too clever for me, uneducated country bumpkin though he undoubtedly is. However, he did ask me to join him to-night in the treasure's final removal, thinking, I guess, that this would

conclusively prove to me the validity of
his find. He doesn't know, of course, that
I have already bought one piece of the set,
and thus know to a certainty that he
speaks the truth.

He came to me, he said, because he had
heard of my interest in old dishes. But
what impudence, if I must say so, for him
to think for one minute that I would con-
nive with him in the exchange of property that was not truthfully his own!
When I thus indignantly attacked him he
brazenly admitted that he had no legal
claim on the silver. But he held out to me
the bait that I could thus add the historic
set to my collection at a fraction of its real
value. I need merely keep my own counsel, he said—though not in those same
words, as his talk, for the most part, was
very coarse and illiterate.

To Al's interests I have let the scoun-
drel believe that I will buy the set for ten
thousand dollars. He is to deliver it to
me to-morrow morning. So there's your
chance! Resourceful as you boys are, and
already on the ground, you certainly
ought to be able to outwit him to-night
when he comes to the island with his spade.
And once you have the treasure in your
possession I would strongly urge that you
immediately start for home.

I might add, for your wider information, that a very excited and vindictive
old gentleman by the name of Benjamin

Clud (not Club, Scoop!) arrived in our
fair village this noon. And what dire
things are to befall me at his revengeful
hands for my interference in his domestic
and financial affairs! But my lawyer as-
sures me that we shall have no trouble disposing of the aforesaid Mr. Clud. So, like
myself, be of good cheer.

Mrs. D.

Gee-miny crickets gosh! Were we ever excited! And Al, of course, with the renewed
prospect of great wealth, was the most excited
of all.

Darkness found us stationed on the north
shore with sharpened ears. Yet at ten o'clock,
to our disappointment and growing anxiety,
we had heard no sound of oarlocks in the surrounding stretch of water. Could it be that
the scheming farm hand had lied to the dish
collector? Had he already removed the silver
from the island? Still, he had invited her to
join him in digging it up. So it must be here.

The moon was up now. And scanning the
northeast shore, where we supposed the Cadman farmhouse to be, we presently caught
sight of a rowboat coming in our direction.
The rower had his back to us. But even at a
distance we could see that he was a big fellow.
And I found myself wondering, as he drew

closer, if our intended plan of rushing him with clubs and rocks would be as successful as we hoped. Plainly, what we needed was a gun. Then, if he refused to throw up his hands and surrender the treasure to its rightful owner, we could blow his head off. But boys of our age aren't supposed to handle guns.

He passed within a hundred feet of us as we lay hidden on the shore by the spring. Landing near the cat-tail marsh he started inland with a spade and bag. We saw him line up a spot between two huge bowlders. But before starting to work he pulled a big revolver from his right hip pocket, placing the gun conspicuously on one of the rocks. Then he unloaded a similar gun from the other hip pocket.

After short work he uncovered a piece of the treasure. We saw him brush it with his jacket sleeve and chuck it into the bag. Then he dug up another piece.

Armed as he was, and plainly on the alert, it was useless for us to think of capturing him. Yet we had no intention of admitting defeat. I guess not! As Al said, when we held guarded counsel behind a gooseberry bush, however suspicious the worker might be of hidden eyes on the island, with its known campers, he probably would have none of these same fears in landing on his own shore. So, if we could beat him home, how easy for us to watch where he hid the treasure, preliminary to its morning delivery, and then snitch it on him.

Unwilling to ask us to share further risks with him, Al would have started out alone in the skiff if I hadn't offered to go along. Rowing to beat the cars, we finally struck the northeast shore where we pulled the skiff into the weeds. Pretty soon we caught sight of the returning farm boat. Then, flattened in the weeds, we watched the man lift the laden sack to his broad back and start off in the direction of the farm buildings a short distance away. Stopping at a small detached shed, which we learned later on was a storehouse for corncobs, he disappeared inside. And when he came out a few minutes later his back was empty.

So we knew, all right, where the treasure was.

CHAPTER XIX

A HOUSE OF STRANGE SECRETS

ALL wrapped up in Al, as you might say, and wanting to help him in every way I could, you can imagine, I guess, how happy I was over the way things were working out. We had met with disappointment in our earlier search for the treasure. But there were to be no disappointments this trip. I guess not! All we had to do now, I figured, was to lay low until the farmer had gone to bed. Then the treasure would be ours. And long before he woke up to the discovery of his loss, we would be back in Tutter, scow and all, pirates no longer, but simply a gang of wildly happy boys.

I had no idea what the treasure actually was worth. We had talked of a hundred thousand dollars. That, probably, was too much. Still, to judge from the way Mrs. Dexter had written to us about the silver it must be worth a great deal more than ten thousand dollars. Possibly thirty thousand dollars. Oh, baby! And here it was within a few feet of our eager hands.

With thirty thousand dollars in the bank Al

would be a rich boy. He could have good
clothes like the rest of us and go to high school
and college. He could have an automobile,
too, when he became old enough to get a
driver's license. And to think that only a few
days ago he was poorer than dirt! Certainly,
I thought, sort of reverent-like, as I coughed
up a bug, this was living proof of God's great
love for boys. Things had looked pretty dark
for Al in his younger years. His pa and ma
had been taken away from him. Left without
a penny, his rich grandma had disowned and
then disinherited him. Strangers had knocked
him around, half feeding and half clothing
him, interested only in what they could get
out of him. Yet, though peculiarly slow to
act, God never had lost sight of him. Not for
one moment. And now the homeless one, after
all of his trials and tribulations, as the Bible
says, was going to get his just reward.

I squeezed his warm hand as I lay beside
him in the weeds, our bodies touching, and he
understood as plainly as spoken words what
I meant. Nor was I at a loss to understand
what *he* meant when he gave my hand an answering squeeze, for I was no gladder over his
good fortune than he was over my friendship
for him.

"Jerry," he broke into my thoughts.

"Yes?" I answered quickly.

"Does it seem to you too good to be true?"

"We *know* it's true, Al," I again pressed his hand.

"It's so *easy*," he said slowly, "that it worries me."

"But why should it worry you?"

"I'm afraid of a trap."

The farmer in the meantime had gone on to the house, an angular stone structure that loomed ghost-like in the moonlight, and we had seen him slip quietly into a side door. Now a light appeared in one of the upper rooms facing the lake.

"He's going to bed," I told my chum.

"I'd sooner think he's secretly watching from one of the other darkened windows."

Yes, and I had the sudden peculiar feeling. as I lay looking at the old house, whose weird history was the whispered talk of the neighborhood, that other spidery-armed things with vapory bodies and venomous eyes were spying at us through those selfsame shadowy windows. *Voodooism!* Its full force was here. The very aspect of the silent house proved it.

Then, as the light went out, I laughed to myself over these silly fears. There was no such thing as spooks—not even spooks conjured up by voodooism. True, Al's grandmother, a known "voodooer," had peculiarly predicted her own death. But that was just a strange coincidence, or whatever you call it. And how foolish for anyone to believe that the queer old lady really could come back from the grave in spirit form. No, sir. When people were put away in the ground that was the end of them. Every time. They might have held to queer supernatural beliefs during their lifetime. But these beliefs amounted to nothing after their death.

The treasure shed, the moonlit door of which conspicuously faced the house, was easily within range of the farmer's guns. So we wisely decided against the risk of an open entrance. Nor did we meet with any immediate success when we crawled up on the shed from behind, depending on it for protection. For it had no windows or a second door. Nor could we detect any loose boards.

Suddenly I stepped into a shallow hole. And away scampered a long four-legged thing in the moonlight.

"Rats!" breathed Al, clutching my arm. Then, with a kind of stifled cry, he dropped to his knees and began digging in the sandy soil with his bare hands. "Look, Jerry! The ground is honeycombed with rat runs."

It was then that we suspected the truth

about the shed: It was a cob house, with a dirt floor. And it was the cobs, many of which contained a few kernels of corn, that attracted the rats.

To get at the treasure, which probably was hidden in the cobs, we decided to pattern after the hungry rats and burrow under the back wall. Nor was this as hard a job as you might imagine. For the ground was soft. And a convenient rubbish pile supplied the needed tools.

Pretty soon we tapped the shed's cob supply, thus proving our theory. And then what should come tumbling down on top of us, as we worked in the hole, but the loaded treasure bag itself. Oh, baby!

It was the silver, all right. We made sure of that. And then, working like snakes, we dragged the heavy bag to the lake shore where we loaded it into the skiff. If the farmer was secretly watching the shed's door from his window, as we still suspected, we certainly had fooled him slick.

All we had to do now was to row the treasure to the island, crank the motor of the old scow and scoot for home, to later celebrate our victory with a few dozen choice banana splits, Al paying the bill. Of course, our adventure, with its successful climax, would be the talk of the town. And those who knew us would go out of their way to rubber at us, as is the case with all heroes, and ask us about this and that, and tell us what smart boys we were. Which would be kind of nice. For a fellow likes to be appreciated. They could even get out the town band, if they wanted to, without hurting my feelings.

But instead of quickly seating himself in the waiting skiff, as I expected of him, Al peculiarly hung back. And I wondered at this.

"Just think, Jerry," he spoke softly, looking back at the farmhouse, "this was my mother's early home. She was born here. And I suppose she used to play up and down this very shore. That was her room in the northeast corner of the house, where you see the big vine. She told me all about it. And that room with the double window was my grandmother's."

I thought of Mrs. Cassidy's story.

"Did you know," I asked him, "that everything in your grandmother's room was left just as it was when she died?"

"No," he shook his head.

"It was her dying wish," I explained. "Shut up right after her death, the room hasn't been opened to this day."

Suddenly he gave a startled cry.

"But, Jerry, that can't be true. For there's a light in her window now."

I had seen the moving light myself. Just as plain as day. And I don't mind telling you that I was scared stiff. For this was a queer house, anyway.

"Quick, Al," I shivered. "Let's get away from here."

"Maybe it's a signal, Jerry," he further held back, as I might have done, too, if it had been *my* grandmother's house. "See! There it is again."

"Come on," I begged.

But I might just as well have tried to move the rock of Gibraltar.

"Jerry, if it *is* a spook, as you think, it must have a *reason* for signaling to us. And if it's a man or a woman I'd like to know what they're doing in my grandmother's room at this time of night."

"It's probably old Cadman," I further shivered.

"The dirty crook!" Al's temper flared up, as he thought of the wrongs that he had suffered at the dishonest farmer's hands. "What right has *he* to go snooping around in my grandmother's room if she ordered it kept closed?"

"Come on, Al. Please."

"Do you suppose it would hold me, Jerry?"

"What?"

"The big vine. My mother told me it was just like a ladder."

"Oh, for the love of mud!" I felt myself slipping. "Are you *crazy?*"

"Jerry, if I go away from here to-night without seeing into that room I'll forever be sorry."

"Yes," I told him, "and if old Cadman or that big guy catches you peeking in the window you'll be a whole lot sorrier, too."

"Something seems to tell me that I *should* do it, Jerry. Didn't you ever have a feeling like that?"

"No," I shook my head, "not *that* kind of a feeling. But it runs in *your* family, I guess."

What we should have done, now that we had the treasure, was to dig for home and *dig quick*. I realized that. To monkey around this way, under the very nose of the farm hand, as you might say, was sheer madness. We were liable to lose everything. But it did no good to argue the matter. For Al was bound and determined to find out what the hated "voodooer" was doing in his grandmother's supposedly sealed bedroom.

And to tell the truth I was kind of curious about it myself. So, having dumped the bag

of silver into the shallow lake, as the quickest
way of hiding it, we guardedly approached the
somber house where we climbed the big vine,
hand over hand, coming at length to the desired window. But the room was in total
darkness. Nor did our sharpened ears pick up
the slightest sound from within. The whole
house seemingly was a well of silence.

That trip up the vine, I think, was the riski-
est stunt I ever pulled off. So I'm not bragging about it. I'm just telling you. The vine,
itself, notwithstanding its iron supports set
into the aged masonry, could easily have
pulled loose under our double weight, thus
dropping us to the ground. More than that
we faced probable dangers from within. Still,
I've never been sorry that I did it.

Al tried the window. And finding it un-
locked he noiselessly raised it.

"Come on, Jerry," he breathed, scrambling
over the sill.

I wasn't going to back out now. Anyway,
he seemed to be safe enough. So in I went,
too, finding myself in a rather large, old-
fashioned room the atmosphere of which was
weighted with a queer stagnant smell. Dead
people! That was it. And there on the
papered wall, dimly lighted by the moon, a
silent reminder of Mrs. Cassidy's spooky

story, was the clock that had stopped so mysteriously the night its mistress died. The bed, too!—the one in which she had breathed her last, thus fulfilling the weird prediction . . . What *was* that smell, anyway? Embalming fluid? Or was it the sickening odor of calla lilies? *Phew!*

Wherever Al went in the carpeted room I followed, hanging to him, the both of us moving on tiptoes. We found two doors, one opening into a closet, filled with dresses, and the other connecting with the hall. This latter door was locked.

His sharp eyes missing nothing in the dimly lighted room, Al gave particular attention to a wall safe, the iron door of which stood open. It was here, no doubt, that his grandmother had kept her private papers. But the safe now was empty.

After looking in the closet we had closed the door, supposedly latching it. But now, as though moved by invisible hands, the door slowly swung open, inch by inch. We watched it with horrified eyes, the more so when it as slowly swung shut. Click! went the latch. Then we caught the faint rustle of a woman's skirts.

Gee-miny crickets gosh! It was Al's grandmother. *Right there in the room with us,* mind you. I never was so scared in all my life.

Bang! A chair fell over. Then we heard a steady tick! tick! tick! The same invisible hand that had opened the closet door had started the clock. Then, as though to completely scare the wits out of us, a key turned in the lock of the hall door.

Before we could squeeze the paralysis out of our icy legs, and escape through the open window, the door opened, admitting an old man in a long white nightshirt. He carried a hand lamp, the light of which gave us a queer picture of his tangled gray hair and aged face. But more than anything else about him we noticed his eyes. Staring and glassy, like a dead man's, they further had a haunted look that was bad for the nerves of anybody who looked into them—a pair of eyes that I'll never forget as long as I live. I saw them only once, but I never want to see them again—certainly, not in *that* room. If this was the stamp of voodooism, deliver me from any such fate as that.

Yes, as you probably have guessed, it was old Mr. Cadman. And when I tell you that he was *hunchbacked* you'll quickly be relieved of further mystery surrounding the identity of Chet Milden's "ghost."

The man either was asleep or acting under some weird supernatural power. For he seemed not to see us at all, though once he looked directly at us. Watching him, we soon learned the truth about the earlier lights that we had seen in the room. For he went directly to the wall safe. Returning something to the safe, he then closed and secured the iron door, after which he turned and left the room, locking the door behind him.

Again that peculiar rustle! It passed us as we crouched against the wall. Then, as before, the closet door opened and closed inch by inch. The rustle was gone!

Tick! . . . tick! . . . tick! . . . The clock stopped.

An hour later we were telling the weird story to our open-mouthed chums on the island. The hunchback, we said, was old Cadman, himself. And it was to him that we must turn for a solution of the mystery surrounding the sealed cave.

CHAPTER XX

ADDED TREASURE

We now had the job on our hands of taking down the tents and otherwise getting things in shape for hasty flight from the island. And as this was easier work than rowing the loaded skiff around the island to the south bay, where the scow was kept, Peg offered to take our place at the oars, figuring, I guess, that both Al and I had done enough hard rowing for one night.

But to our amazement the tents were gone. And so was the scow. Bid Stricker's work, of course. The blamed sneak! He hadn't gone home at all. That was just a smart trick. And how lovely for him that we had left our camp and scow unguarded!

Gosh! If this wasn't a mess. Just when we needed the old scow the most it was gone, having evidently been towed away to the enemy's secret camp. To our added misfortune the skiff sprung a leak on its trip around the island, the hard-working rower having rammed into a submerged bowlder. So further use of the water-logged craft was out of

the question. As for our raft, we found that
it, too, had been lugged off.

Seemingly the only course left open to us
was to stay right where we were. Which
would mean a later battle with the Strickers.
But that didn't worry us. The way we felt
now we were equal in strength and grit to a
hundred of Bid's kind. Gr-r-r-r! If ever a
guy needed a good beating it was him.

As for the burly farm hand, we could only
hope that he would carry his search for the
vanished silver any place else except back to
the island. Still, it would be a miracle if he
didn't descend on us with those two big guns
of his. For the hole under the treasure shed
was unmistakably boys' work. And who else
would he be more liable to suspect than us?

Fortunately Bid and his marauders had
over-looked our torches, stored in the hollow
tree with the pirate clothes. And determined
now to hide the treasure in the depths of the
big cave we accordingly loaded our arms from
the opened sack and started out. At the
mouth of the cave we lit a torch apiece, carrying it as best we could. Then, entering single
file, with Peg in the lead, we followed the long
sloping corridor, with its dripping walls and
shallow pools, coming at length to the big pool
at the bottom of the incline. Here there was

loose sand. And digging with the silver plates, themselves, the only "shovels" available, we soon scooped out a sizable hole.

Suddenly Al gave a cry that echoed weirdly through the rock-domed chamber.

"Look, fellows! See what I found. Another silver dish."

"What?" cried Scoop, sharing the other's excitement. "Did you dig it up?"

"Sure thing."

Peg then gave a similar cry.

"And here's another. Hot diggity! I can see three more, too. The sand is full of them."

Well, if ever the world contained a gang of amazed boys it was us. The spring seemingly had held only half of the silver. The other half had been hidden in the cave. Still, much was left unexplained. For the dishes, we noticed, lowering our smoking torches for closer investigation, were unmistakably different.

What the dickens? . . . Were there two separate sets? It would seem so. We turned to Al for light on the subject. But he threw up his hands, telling us, with a dizzy look, that he was as mystified as we were.

We counted the pieces of the first set. Eleven plates, twelve cups, and in general twelve of everything, except the bowls and platters. Yet, after an hour's work, we had

another set of the same number of pieces.
And, as I have said, there was a noticeable
difference in the pattern.

It was a cinch, as Scoop said, that both sets
couldn't be the King's Silver. Yet how amazing that an additional set had been hidden on
the island. We were completely dumfounded.

But it was all added good luck for Al. For
now he was doubly rich. Or, if it turned out
that only one of the sets was his, *we* would be
rich, too. Thirty thousand dollars divided by
four. Almost eight thousand dollars apiece.
Oh, baby! Greater luck could hardly be imagined. I'd give Mother a thousand dollars, for
I had heard her say that she wanted a new
parlor set. I'd buy something swell for Dad,
too. Maybe a new car. Just imagine a boy
of my age doing that! And I'd still have thousands of dollars left.

The silver was put together in one big hole,
after which (so we thought!) we cleverly concealed all traces of our work. Then, with the
bats zipping around our heads, attracted by
our flaming torches, of which we lighted new
ones from our supply as soon as the others
burned out, we went back up the corridor to
the smaller cave, where we spent the balance
of the night, one standing guard while the
others slept crosswise in the jailed Bible

peddler's bed, the cave furnishings having been undisturbed.

There was food here, too, so we didn't go hungry the following morning. During breakfast we heard the sound of our old motor, and later, from under cover, we saw Bid and his chesty gang land on the south shore. As in the "Whispering Cave" book they had armed themselves with bows and arrows. Getting sight of us, the battle started. And for a short time we held them off with stones. In the end, though, we had to retreat to the cave. Here we later surrendered, gálling as it is to me to admit it, for old Clud, direct from Tutter, had joined them, armed with a revolver.

Later they found the treasure, suspecting from our burned torches that something had been buried there. The cave rang with their triumphant shouts as piece after piece was uncovered. As for us, bound hand and foot as we were, and threatened with even worse punishment by the vindictive old miser, our misery was complete. I'm telling it briefly. For even to this day I hate to think about it.

And then, while they were quarreling over the loot at the mouth of the cave, old Clud greedily trying to grab every other piece, who should come steaming into the wide waters but Mr. Cliffe and his party of campers.

Clud tried to hurry us into the cave. But the newcomers heard us. Nor did the Strickers succeed in escaping with a single piece of the double treasure. Defeated one minute, and in bitter despair, we were hilariously victorious the next.

CHAPTER XXI

NEARING THE END

WHICH really brings me to the end of my story. For, with the men on our side, chief among them the island's owner, himself, we had no trouble getting the treasure home, our other stuff included, though the story of our adventures filled the campers with wonder and amazement.

Realizing that the jig was up, as the saying is, Clud skinned out for Indiana and never since has he bothered Al in the slightest. The latter was adopted by the wealthy Tutter woman, who has set aside a trust fund for him in the amount of twenty-five thousand dollars. So no one can say that she adopted the orphan just to gain possession of the valuable silver. No, sir. She did it because she sensibly wanted a boy in the house. And, bu-lieve me, she has a real one. To-day Al is one of the happiest kids in town. And Mrs. Dexter, whom he calls "ma," the same as he calls Mrs. Cassidy "grandma," thinks that the sun rises and sets in him. While he, in turn, thinks that the sun rises and sets in *me*. Which shows

244

you—ahem—that he's a kid of rare good sense.

Shortly after the adoption papers were made out, Mrs. Dexter told Dad that she was going to start suit against the aged farmer to try and make him give up the wide-waters farm to its rightful owner. But before the case came up in court the old man died. His conscience literally killed him, I guess. Or maybe, having cheated the grandson out of his inheritance, he stood in deadly fear of what the grandmother's wrathful "spirit" might do to him. Mrs. Morrison may have resented her daughter's marriage. And, in a hard-hearted moment, she may further have torn up the letter that the daughter wrote, begging for help. But I don't think the old lady ever intended to disinherit the grandson. She gave him five years to show up and claim his inheritance. And, to that point, we know why he didn't show up within the prescribed five-year period.

Still, Mr. Cadman wasn't a truthfully bad man. His greed simply got the best of him, which should be a good lesson for all of us. He left a will (which was one of the papers that we saw him lock up in the wall safe) by the terms of which everything was returned to the wronged grandson. And he begged for forgiveness. So let us hope that his soul rests in peace. I never will believe, though, like some of the superstitious people in that neighborhood, that he was killed by a vindictive spirit. Queer strings and hidden wires were later uncovered in the grandmother's death chamber. So it was plain to everybody concerned that a lot of the "strange power" that she claimed for herself was faked. "Mediums" do that. And I don't think that the trickery of the old lady's was such a strange thing. She just wanted to be a mystery to her inquisitive neighbors. When the wires were removed from under the carpet the clock and closet door properly behaved themselves. Still, I'd hate to sleep in that room. I'd always have queer fears.

The other day I saw an article in the newspaper telling about a man who not only accurately predicted his own death but had fitted himself out with a coffin. Nothing was said about voodooism. So, I guess, what Mrs. Morrison did in the way of predicting her own death wasn't anything new. Some queer things happen in this world. And when a fellow brushes up against anything out of the ordinary his imagination sort of leads him on, as ours did the night we heard the "rustling dress." That, Dad declares, was pure imagination.

So we thus dispose of Mr. Cadman's part in the story. He did wrong, repented on his deathbed, and later everything was made right. How he managed to leave the island unseen the day Chet saw the "ghost" is unimportant. We know why he came to the island. It was to seal up the cave, a hiding place for his own hoardings, which later were recovered and turned over to his relatives. A peculiar man, surely. But the world contains many such.

And now I come to Arnold Peters, whose real name was Peter Gormany. A widely known swindler, who pocketed many thousands of dishonest dollars yearly through the sale of fake "antiques," he had set a clever trap for Mrs. Dexter. Having heard of the King's Silver, and also of the wealthy Tutter collector, he searched the eastern second-hand stores until he found a silver set suitable for his purpose. With the set in his possession he then dressed up like a farm hand and came to our section, hiring out on the Cadman farm. It was his intention to bury the set on the island, later secretly reporting his "find" to the dish collector. He had worked similar schemes on other collectors. Once, while in England, after renting an old house, he had "found" an unknown manuscript of William Shakespeare's in a hidden drawer in an old desk. In the current scheme it was his intention to go to Mrs. Dexter with one of the fake plates, posing as a rube, telling her that he had "dug up" the plate on the island. She, of course, would quickly associate the plate with the long-lost silver. So how easy for him to "recover" the balance of the set. Or, if he could get her to help him dig it up, so much the better. In either event he figured that her eagerness to possess the historic set would help him out. And, to that point, if unable to do better, he was prepared to sell for as little as one thousand dollars, which was nine hundred dollars more than the set had cost him.

Hiding in the dish collector's barn the day I stopped there, he thus learned, by the aid of his sharp ears, that we were headed for the island. So he decided not to present his plate that day, figuring that he might be able to cook up some scheme of letting *us* find the treasure, which would make its recovery seem still more convincing. Listening at the old tavern, he had overheard Al's story of the vanished diary. The very thing! That night he faked a diary—a comparatively easy job for one who had earlier faked a Shakespearean play! And having noticed an old trunk in an outbuilding at the farm, he lugged this, clothes and all, to the tavern, where, as we know, he "hid" the trunk in the attic, confident of its later "discovery." Then he dropped the one plate into the spring, figuring that upon its recovery our first thought would be to sell it to our Tutter friend, after which, of course, he could quickly appear (which he did) and claim to have hidden the balance of the treasure in another spot. The stuff about Mr. Cadman "talking in his sleep" was all made up.

Certainly, a clever scheme. And it might have worked if Mrs. Dexter's friendship for us hadn't outweighed her collecting eagerness, as you might say.

The set that we found in the cave was the real King's Silver, put there years and years ago by Al's great-grandmother, who either got into the known cave through the "window" or through a now submerged entrance. The "fake" set was taken away by the law.

The swindler tried to get away, but a detective who long had been on his trail caught him in Chicago. And that was the end of *him*.

Which brings me to the wind-up of my story. But before you put this book aside, suppose you turn to the next page and read my "addenda," which, I venture to say, contains information that will greatly interest you.

CHAPTER XXII

DAD sells paving bricks all over the United
States. And quite often he goes away on long
business trips. On one of these recent eastern
trips he stopped over in New York City to see
the people who publish my books, the Grosset
and Dunlap Company, and right away, of
course, they asked about *me*.

Well, Dad had a big story to tell them. I
was one of the four proud owners of a husky
young elephant, he said, given to us by a rich
uncle of Red Meyers'. And it was nip and
tuck with us to find enough for the elephant
to eat.

Which was no fish story, let me tell you. I
guess not! I never saw anything that could
beat that elephant when it came to eating. We
pretty nearly broke our backs cutting grass for
it. In one day, extra of the grass that we cut
with two lawn mowers, it ate three dozen
bananas and fifteen oranges (skins and all), a
peck of apples (cores and all), a bushel of car-
rots, a pumpkin pie, a peck of chicken feed,
four hunks of cake, eight cheese sandwiches and

250

three loaves of bread. And then, for dessert, it finished off with Red's ma's imported grass porch rug, which was the particular thing that got us in bad at 1014 Main Street, for Mrs. Meyers, who still tells how mortified she was the day we brought the elephant home while she was entertaining the Stitch and Chatter Club, was furious over the loss of her Japanese rug. She even called our nice elephant a family nuisance. Which shows you how unreasonable some mothers can be when their tempers get away from them. As though the porch rug or the old club meeting was half as important as our swell elephant! But we couldn't make her see it that way at all.

Well, Dad told the whole story to Grosset and Dunlap—how the elephant, at sight of a mouse, pushed the back out of Red's garage, which turned Mr. Meyers against us, also, the repair bill coming to over a hundred dollars, and how Red and Bingo later ran away in the dark. We helped the runaway get his stuff together. And what a mess of junk it was! About what you'd expect of Red Meyers. No wonder poor Bingo's legs spraddled out before he had gone a mile.

But what interested the book publisher as much as the fun that we were having with our nice elephant, giving programs and so on, was the bewildering mystery of Henny Bibbler. And right away, with an eye to business, the general manager of the company instructed Dad to have me put the whole story down on paper so that it could be made into a book to be called JERRY TODD AND THE BOB-TAILED ELEPHANT.

I was further instructed, through Dad, to write an "addenda" about the proposed new book, to be printed in the back of this book, as the publisher seemed to think that the boys who read my books would be glad to know what was coming. Well, to be frank, I didn't know whether an "addenda" was something that you ate with a soup spoon or a scalp disease. So I got out my trusty dictionary, thus learning that an "addenda" is a sort of extra caboose. After the train is all made up, so to speak, with the cowcatcher in front and the regular caboose behind, a second caboose is hitched on at the very tail end, and this is the "addenda."

Or, in other words, an "addenda" is something "additional."

So here is my "addenda." And, as I have mentioned, its purpose is to put you wise to the coming hilarious story of the funny bob-tailed elephant and Henny Bibbler, "the boy who vanished."

Until *we* took hold of the mystery no one

ever knew the truth about Henny's disappearance. Some people said he ran away from home. Others said the spooks got him.

You see, Henny lived with his ma on a little farm just north of town in Happy Hollow One cold, crispy evening in January he started for the spring to get a pail of water. "Hurry back, Henny," his ma told him, in her kindly, talkative way, as she bustled about the cozy kitchen, "for the johnnycake is in the oven." Henny loved johnnycake. And on the way to the outside door he stopped at the oven to peek in. You can imagine how tempting the johnnycake looked to him. For almost any kind of warm food looks tempting to a boy after he has been skating for two or three hours. "Um-yum," said he, patting his stomach. "Johnnycake and honey." Then out through the door he went on the tear.

His ma later told the story that she set out to look for him when he didn't come back. His tracks in the new snow led straight toward the spring. But he never reached the spring, which was covered with ice several hours old. Suddenly the tracks ended, Henny seemingly having walked off into space.

The newspapers made a big story of the strange disappearance. And people who believed in spooks came for miles around to listen at the spring. For Mrs. Bibbler told the further amazing story that she frequently heard Henny's muffled voice in the air. When asked what he said she couldn't give any words. She was dead sure, though, that it was his voice. The neighbors frequently saw her walking up and down the path that he took that fatal night. She'd take a step or two, then stop and listen. One day she stayed out so long that she frosted her feet. *She* knew that there was some weird mystery surrounding Henny's disappearance. And she couldn't rest easy.

Was the vanished one really trapped in an "air pocket," invisible to us yet constantly near us? The queer old detective who was sent to Tutter to investigate the amazing disappearance, undoubtedly the strangest case we ever tackled as Juvenile Jupiter Detectives, told us a lot of scientific stuff about "air pockets." Later our elephant's tail disappeared; and then the animal's whole body, trunk and all. Seemingly added proof of the "air-pocket" theory.

Remember the title, JERRY TODD AND THE BOB-TAILED ELEPHANT. A big book packed full of skylarking fun and baffling mystery. And it's coming soon.

THE END

"HOT OFF THE GRIDIRION" STORIES

Football at Its Best and Most Exciting!

UNDER THE GOAL POSTS
by Eddie Dooley

●

JIMMY MAKES THE VARSITY
by Jonathan Brooks

●

By Harold M. Sherman

ONE MINUTE TO PLAY

TOUCHDOWN!

BLOCK THAT KICK!

CRASHING THROUGH!

FIGHT 'EM, BIG THREE

GOAL TO GO!

HOLD THAT LINE!

NUMBER 44

●

GROSSET & DUNLAP

Publishers   **NEW YORK**

On the Trail of Clues and Criminals!

THE
HARDY BOYS STORIES

By Franklin W. Dixon

Frank and Joe Hardy are sons of a celebrated detective. Often the boys help him in his investigations. In their spare hours and during vacations they follow up clues "on their own hook." These activities lead them into many strange and dangerous adventures in stories that are packed with action, suspense and mystery.

GROSSET & DUNLAP

Publishers   NEW YORK

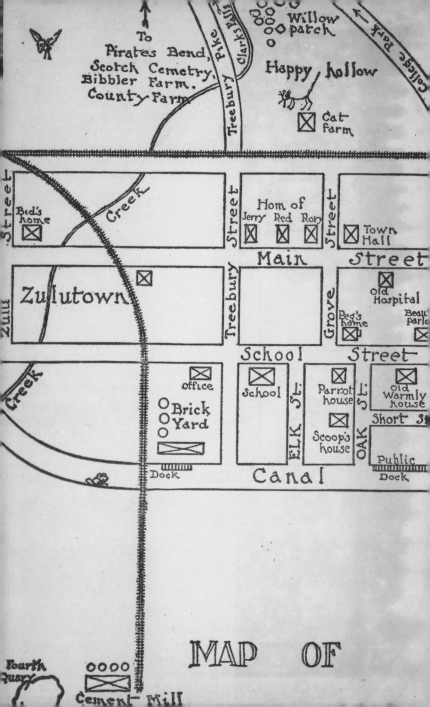